WEEKEND WITH RYLIE

WEEKEND SERIES: BOOK ONE

K.M. RINGER

Kimberly M. Ringer

CONTENT WARNING

THIS BOOK CONTAINS REFERENCES TO DOMESTIC VIOLENCE, ON PAGE GUN VIOLENCE, ANXIETY ATTACKS, PANIC ATTACKS, AND CONTAINS INSTANCES OF PTSD FLASHBACKS.

# Dedication

To anyone who just needs loved unconditionally
and
fucked beyond all comprehension

CONTENTS

CHAPTER ONE

I slammed my book shut in frustration. GOD! I just can't concentrate. How many times had I read that page? Ten? Twelve? I looked out the window and we must be somewhere over the Rockies. When I left the Bay Area for Chicago, I was bubbling with excitement. It had been three long weeks since I had seen Rylie. He had come out to visit, but I hadn't been out to Chicago to see him in almost three months. Because of this, I had added a few extra vacation days to the business trip to spend with him. He had arranged for additional time off, but said he may have to take calls from time to time.

I was meeting my boss for the hopeful signing of a very high-profile contract. The Henderson and Sons contract would lock us into multiple construction projects over the next ten to twenty years. It would also propel my career if I could convince Mr. Henderson to sign on the dotted line tomorrow.

Two weeks ago, I had been in Houston for a week, and there was hardly a moment I wasn't in a meeting with those clients. Sam Bradford, my boss, had only arranged a few in-person meetings for this trip, but if Ray Henderson signed, I would not be surprised if tomorrow ended up being a very long day. The good news was that afterwards I would be mostly free to do what I wished while here.

I didn't mind the trips. Chicago allowed me time with Rylie without him having to get time off and fly out to California, which he did as often as he could get away. In Houston, if there was time, the trip gave me the ability to see some friends and family.

Sam had me scheduled to work for three days in Chicago before taking a few days off. I still wasn't sure how I had convinced Sam to allow me to take the vacation time. Once this contract was signed, it was going to be a mad rush in drafting and finalizing the drawings. Henderson and Sons already had construction crews on standby to hopefully break ground in four months. Getting it pushed through building and planning was going to be a chore, and I could feel the stress filling my shoulders just thinking about it.

A smile lifted my lips as I thought of how I could relieve the stress. Rylie. I shifted in my seat, and the lady next to me asked, "Nervous?"

I was, but not for the reason she was asking. "Of flying? No. I fly pretty often."

She nodded and then went back to her book. I smiled as I recognized the title. "You enjoying it?"

"I am. It's not everyone's cup of tea." She lowered her voice a bit and said, "I love some good cliterature, and I'll be seeing my boyfriend for the first time in four months, so he will reap the benefits." She grinned, reaching up and touching her necklace.

"I bet he will." I smiled at her.

"You've read it?"

"I have. Wait until you get to the kitchen table scene." I winked at her.

"Read that about ten minutes ago. The author did a great job describing how it felt to go down the throat from the male's perspective, didn't she?"

The younger man on the aisle seat shifted, and I leaned forward to see him blushing. Smirking, I met the woman's eye, and smiled. "She did. Takes talent to take a man like that. Not every woman can do it right. Have to get the right angle."

She hummed in agreement, and the guy shifted in his seat and tried to readjust himself. I whispered, "I think we are making him uncomfortable."

She chuckled, "Regardless, it's a good book. Sir required me to read it on the plane. Said something about the office scene becoming reality."

I smiled broadly at her, recalling that scene. I gave her a chef's kiss before I cocked my head to the side and nodded at the necklace she wore. "He'll be pleased."

Her hand flew to the leather choker with the small metal ring on the front. A blush rose to her cheeks, and it was the only confirmation I needed, but she said, "Sir will be happy indeed".

I smiled, but then sighed. I wanted to have that conversation with Rylie, but it would be really difficult long distance. "I'll let you get back to it. Don't want to let your man down."

She smiled as she looked at the book in my lap. I still had a few more hours on the plane, so I picked up the book and tried again.

I PULLED MY PHONE out, looking at the time. 4:40 p.m. local, and with the press of a few buttons, opened the messenger:

Luci:
Just landed. Meet me at the hotel at 7.

Rylie:
You brought what I instructed?

Luci:
Yes.

Rylie:
Put it in and send me a photo.

Luci:
Aren't you supposed to be sleeping?

Rylie:
Couldn't sleep. Do I have to repeat myself? You have five minutes.

I sighed and headed to the bathroom. After having to wait a moment for a free stall, I was pleased to see it allowed enough room for me to open my carry on just enough to slip out the silicone butt plug and lube. Security had only raised a slight eyebrow at the items when they searched my bag. One of them had even smirked a little. My phone went off, and I saw a message from Rylie.

One minute.

Sighing, I squeezed the bottle to apply a small bit of lube on the tip, then slowly inserted it in. I bit back a moan, and when I stood, I wiggled a bit to ensure it wouldn't fall out walking. Then I took my phone and proved to him I had followed directions.

Rylie:
Good girl. Don't remove it until you see me.

Luci:
I have a dinner meeting with Sam.

Rylie:
I know.

Luci:
That isn't fair.

Rylie:
Who said I play fair? I'll see you soon.
I could have picked you up, but you refused to give me the flight info.

There were two reasons I didn't give him the flight info. The first was that I knew he had to sleep. Rylie had been in some stressful meetings the last few days, and I knew he would be wiped out. This was the start of a five-day vacation for him, and I wanted to make sure he was well rested. The second reason, of course, was because I knew I would have to meet with Sam for dinner, and I didn't want to see him, only to have to leave him so soon.

I closed up the carryon, flushed the toilet, and after adjusting the dress I had on to ensure everything was indeed covered, I strode out and washed my hands.

When my phone started ringing, I rushed out of the bathroom and answered it. "Luci Baker."

"Hey Luci."

"Sam." I moved over to a corner so I could hopefully hear him better. "I just got in."

"That's why I'm calling. My kid is sick. Can we just meet in the morning? My wife won't be home for a few more hours."

I blinked. "Sure. 9:00 am at the office?"

"Sounds good. See you then. Sorry for the change of plans." Then he hung up as I heard hacking coughs in the background.

I headed down to where the taxis were and pulled my black lightweight sweater tighter around me. I can't believe I agreed to wear this dress to travel. I had tried to tell Rylie that it would be too cold, but he had just chuckled and ordered me to wear the spaghetti strapped, corseted sundress, with a lightweight black sweater, and the anklet he gave me. The necklace wasn't specified, but it looked great with the dress.

Granted, I looked good. I'd worked hard at the gym, and the muscle definition that I had created really showed well in this dress. While I still had about ten pounds I wanted to lose, it had been a long road to get where I was, and I was proud of that. I would never be that thin model type, but I was okay with it. I had muscle and curves, and Rylie certainly enjoyed running his hands along each ripple of them. In fact, he had seemed to revel in me accepting my body. He would often go out of his way to make me feel like a million dollars.

I took a deep breath and started to absently play with the charm on my necklace as I made my way down. My phone buzzed, and when I checked, it was my best friend, Katie. She had been so smug and difficult about this trip. She had told me to make sure to look left when I got to the taxi line up. That girl had always had the best intuition. Hell, I would go as far as to say Katie could straight see the future, but we would just be called crazy for that. I chuckled at the short, quick message.

Katie the PIMA BFF:
Have fun, and don't forget left at the taxis.

I stepped on the escalator down to the taxi and pickup area, and thought about calling Rylie to have him just come get me. The only problem with that was I would have to wait here. At least at the hotel, I could be comfortable. Well, as comfortable as I could be until he showed up. Either way, I would be a mess of nerves.

I stepped off the escalator, and instinctively did as Katie requested. She had never steered me wrong, and so I looked left. Blinked, and did a double take.

Chapter Two

"That fucking bitch." I whispered. How could she hold out information like this? I took a few steps to get out of the way, and froze again, when I saw Rylie take a deep breath, run his hand over his face, put his ball cap back on, and flipped the hood of his hoodie over the top. He leaned his head back and closed his eyes for a moment, his phone fisted tightly in his hand while tapping it on his leg. He hadn't noticed me standing here like an idiot yet.

I couldn't help but stare at him. He was all hard muscle and sex incarnate. I realized my eyes had filled with tears even with the huge smile on my face. That was the moment that Rylie Allen looked in my direction and pushed off the wall. His eyes trailed up and down the length of me, licked his lips, and then slowly lifted his hand and curved his finger for me to come to him.

I was practically running by the time I reached him and when I threw my arms around his neck, Rylie picked me up and swung me around. When his lips met mine,

I moaned in relief. My body instantly relaxed, and I couldn't help but shiver under his touch.

When he pulled back, he held my waist tight, refusing to put me down. "You lied to me."

"I didn't lie. I said I couldn't sleep."

"You said you would see me... soon." I whispered against his lips, realizing the loophole he had left himself, but he just pressed his lips to mine again, letting them linger a moment.

"And I did. I couldn't wait to see you. I called Katie and after a bit of pestering, she gave me the flight information. She knew I would be meeting you here at the airport, and was dramatic in only the ways that Katie could be, and gave it to me."

I smirked at him. "You going to put me down?"

"I like you against me." His voice was full of so much heat that I couldn't think through anything going on in my head. "I love you."

"I love you, too." I said, kissing him again quickly. His eyes were bright, but heated, as he set me down.

"Any checked baggage?" He asked before grabbing my carryon for me.

"No. Everything I need is in there and right here." I tipped my head toward my carryon, smiled, wrapped my arm around his waist, and pressed against him.

"Me, too." Rylie kissed the top of my head. The six inches of height difference was something that some thought was adorable, but I found annoying. Mostly because he would just hold something above my head if I want it, and watched me jump as I struggled to reach it.

As we headed for the parking lot, I noticed he kept his head down, keeping his face partially covered by his ball cap and hood of the sweatshirt. His eyes kept shifting from side to side, and looking over his shoulder as if he was trying to keep from being seen. There was a moment where his eyes met someone's, but then he lowered his head, tipping it to the side, more like he was trying to avoid someone.

"Everything okay?"

"Of course. I have my girl. Nothing could be better." He gave me a quick kiss on the top of my head again, and when I noticed a door ajar on the first level near the elevators, I slowed my pace. My eyes flicked to it a couple of times before we reached it, and when we did, I pulled him inside, locking the door behind us. The janitor's closet wasn't big, but it was big enough.

I pushed him against the wall, and slid my hands up under his shirt, just letting my fingers feel the muscles underneath.

"Rylie. Are you sure everything's okay?" I whispered as I pressed my body against him. His hardness pressed against me, and it was hard not to squirm against it. I took a deep breath and stared him down.

His hand came up to cradle my cheek, as he answered with a soft kiss and a whispered, "I have you at my side, and I can't wait until we are back at the hotel when I can be buried deep inside you again."

"That can be partially arranged." I let my fingers fall to the rough leather of his belt, and quickly freed him from his jeans, before instantly dropping to my knees before him.

"Luci, are you serious right now?" He growled as my tongue flicked through the slit of him. The bead of pre-cum trailing from the head of him to my tongue. He tipped his head back against the wall when I took him into my mouth and sucked softly.

Quickly running my tongue on that spot just under the head, his whole body twitched. I looked up and met his eyes as I took him more fully in and grabbed hold of the base of him. After a few strokes, his hand cradled my head, and he growled, "Such a good girl."

My pussy clenched at the words, and I moaned into him. I felt him twitch and swallowed him. Rylie cradled my head as I held him down my throat, and he laced his fingers in my hair. I bobbed a few times, before coming up for air, licked and swirled the head. He gave me a small smirk before he thrusted himself down my throat, and held me there.

I stretched my tongue out, licked his balls and fingered that spot before reaching his ass. I wiggled and felt the plug move within me. I couldn't help another moan escaping as a wave of pleasure flowed through me.

"Fuck." Was Rylie's only reply and my only warning before he pulled from me and started deep throat fucking me. Over and over again, he thrusted into me, and when I grabbed his ass, there would be small short thrusts, before longer faster ones.

I could feel his cock twitching against my tongue, and when I moaned again, Rylie grunted, "Swallow every drop, sweetheart," as he unloaded himself down my throat.

When I looked up at him, he merely said with a small smile on his face, "Lick me clean."

I smirked at him and did as he commanded. Slowly, I put him away and zipped up his pants, licking my lips. "Hi, hun."

"That is one way to say hello." His eyes trailed over my face, as he reached up and wiped away where my eyeliner had run. "Let's not make it fully apparent what you just did when we walk out of this room."

I just shrugged. "I don't care. Let the world see that I will please my man anywhere. Even an airport janitorial closet."

Rylie pulled my chin up and leaned down, pressing his lips to mine, letting his lips linger a moment before pulling away. "Fucking hell. I love you."

"I love you, too." I winked at him, and at his questioning gaze, I said, "Oh, and by the way, my meeting tonight was canceled. I'm all yours until I have to leave for the meeting at 9:00 a.m."

His eyes widened, and then he blinked a few times. "Well let's get you settled, then. I refuse to lose one single moment alone with you."

CHAPTER THREE

When we walked out of that closet, there was an elderly couple walking by who stopped short when they saw us. While the woman looked at us a moment too long, her husband just smiled. I saw a very specific look in his eye that made me smile broadly and reach up to wipe at the corner of my mouth.

Rylie, on the other hand, chuckled, and then smacked my ass, making that plug move again. I shuddered at the pleasurable pain. The evil look in his eye made me realize just how much I was in for over the next few days.

That was emphasized when we reached the car, and he put my carry on in the back seat, and opened the door for me.

"New car?"

"Old one died. Figured, since I'm doing so well at work right now, I deserved a nicer car." He looked me up and down and shrugged. "I want to drive my girl around in style."

I went to get in, but he just pushed me against the door, trailed his hand up my skirt, and around to where the plug sat. There was a quick glance around the garage before he said, "Hands on the seat."

I bent over and followed his instructions as he lifted my dress and got to his knees. I shifted my hips to allow him a better view of me, and there was a needy groan from him that made me smile. His hands roamed over both of my ass cheeks before smacking one hard. A small chuckle flowed over me at my answering moan.

He spread my legs apart, moved my panties to the side, and trailed a finger from one end of me to the other. "Mmm. Beautifully presented Luci."

"It's all yours." I said as his fingers started working my clit, in small slow movements, but it was when he twisted the butt plug, that I jumped and twitched.

"Yes, it is. Don't you forget it."

"You could remind me just how much you own it." I said just before his tongue ran the length of me and I had to bite my lip to keep from moaning so loud it echoed throughout the garage.

His tongue licked and explored every inch of exposed flesh. I ground and twisted my hips against him as he grasped onto my hips and bit down on my clit. I didn't hold back that time. Rylie smacked my ass, which I was sure was supposed to be his way to remind me to stay quiet, but had quite the opposite effect.

When his tongue entered me, he pulled and pushed the butt plug causing me to grind against him. I was so close. Had been so close since the moment I had first taken him into my mouth in that closet.

Rylie knew it too, because he pulled away, just as I was about to career off that edge, blew on my clit and smacked it.

"Rylie." I begged.

"Not until we get to the hotel." He stood, twisting that plug again, which had me physically concentrating on not cumming at the movement.

"Then you better not move that plug again, because I won't be able to stop myself. Again. It's going to be hard enough to sit in the car." I glared at him as I stood up.

The left side of his lips were lifted in a pleased smile, and it was his eyes that had so much heat, it melted the silver in them.

Resting my hand on his cheek, I stared into those light gray eyes that had captivated me almost two years ago for a long moment before he leaned forward and kissed me hard, gripping my ass and lifting me off the ground. I moaned into him, because again, as that plug moved, it hit that spot. If he wasn't careful, he was going to have a mess on those leather seats.

When I pulled back, our foreheads resting on each other, he growled and said, "Then let's go."

He put me down, and when I slid into the front seat, his eyes trailed up and down my body before meeting my eyes, shaking his head, and closing the door.

"What?" I asked tentatively when he got behind the wheel and turned the car on.

His eyes narrowed. "Huh?"

"Why did you shake your head?" I was suddenly feeling very self-conscious about... well, everything. "Do you not like the dress? Did I do something?"

"What?" He said confused, pulling out of the garage and into the street.

I looked down at my lap and just played with my fingers. "Nothing."

We were about five minutes from the airport when he reached over and put his hand on my thigh. His thumb running in small motions back and forth.

"What's wrong?" Rylie asked when we exited the highway ten minutes later and were sitting at a light. I shook my head and just looked out the window. Rylie let out a long breath and reached over and grabbed my chin, turning me to look at him. "What is going through that head of yours?"

"Why did you shake your head before getting in the car? Did I do something to upset you? Do you not like the dress? Are you mad I pulled you into the closet? Was I too noisy in the garage?" I mumbled, feeling my heart in my throat.

"Lucille Adaline Baker." His voice was a grumbling reprimand, and I instantly shrank down. "Oh, for fuck's sake." He said, grabbing me by the neck and pulling me in for a kiss. It was heated, demanding, and all things dominating. I couldn't help but fall into it.

A car honked behind us, and I pulled back. His fingers gripped tighter on my neck as he pulled me back to him and kissed me. The car honked again, and he smiled before turning back to the road and going through the light.

"Why do you think I could be mad at you?"

"You shook your head, and it was the way you sighed when you closed the door at the garage." My voice was small and tentative, because now I was rethinking everything I'd just said to him. There was nothing in that kiss that felt like I had angered him. But I couldn't shake that something was still wrong.

"I was trying to convince myself to not take you right there. I was exercising self-control." He breathed.

Every horrible, violent memory of Justin flashed through my head. The condescension, the belittling, and everything I did, it was never enough. Every memory went through my head.

"You just wait until we get to the hotel, because I am going to show you just how perfect you are to me and wipe away every shadow that just went across your face forever."

My head snapped to his. "You are supposed to be watching the road, Rylie. Not me."

"Sweetheart, don't forget I know you. I saw you with that fucking asshole, and I saw every twitch you would make when he would degrade and belittle you. I had to stand by and watch as he shredded away the self-worth you had. The only reason I didn't put him in an early grave for it was because you had explicitly asked us to stay out of it. If any of us knew he had been physically hurting you..." He took a deep breath and gripped the wheel tighter.

"On that subject, were you always just standing in the wind, waiting for us to separate?" I asked, half turning toward him.

I pulled myself up and crossed a leg under me, concentrating on ignoring the butt plug because it hit that spot inside me that made me have to close my eyes and breathe. When I opened them, Rylie took my hand, squeezed it, and smirked. "Another twenty minutes, Luce, and I promise I'll let you cum. Until then, you gotta hold off."

"Yes, Rylie." I rolled my eyes.

"As for your other question, no. I wasn't that guy, Luci." He took a deep breath and said, "I've always thought you beautiful, but you were with Justin. I was with Shannon. We were friends, and that was that. Doesn't mean that as your friend at the time, I didn't see what he was doing to you. I just had no right to intervene."

He let out a heavy sigh, and turned down another main road toward a cluster of taller buildings. I'd only ever been to Chicago a couple of times before, and had always taken a taxi, so actually getting to the downtown area? Yeah, I was completely lost, and had no idea where we were going.

"About a year after Shannon and I separated, I moved out here. You had been rid of Justin a few months prior, and I knew you needed the time and space to heal. As we continued to talk on the phone and when I came out to visit our friends, feelings grew. The more we talked, the more I wanted to be the person you came to for everything. When you agreed to go on a real date with me, I... I can't explain how hard it was not to get my hopes up." He stopped at a light, and then looked at me squarely. "To be by your side as you have gone through all that therapy to work on bettering yourself, to reprogram all that horrible shit he had put in that beautiful brain of yours, has been a pleasure. I've watched how hard you work, and I couldn't be more proud of you, Luci."

I rolled my eyes dramatically, and when the light turned green, he shook his head. "Believe me or not, but you are one of the most amazing creatures to walk this earth. I have never wanted anyone more than I want you, Luci."

I looked out the window and watched all the store fronts pass by without a word. Rylie took my hand in my lap and threaded his fingers through mine. After driving a few more blocks, he was pulling into the parking garage under the sandstone hotel I had stayed at for the last few trips. The Chicago office, firmly located within the Business District, was only a few blocks from the hotel, and the coffee shop on the corner was a complete godsend first thing in the morning.

When he parked, he didn't get out right away. Rylie stared at the wall for a long moment. I squeezed his hand and asked, "What are you thinking about?"

"How if I ever saw Justin, I may end up wearing orange for a long time for what he did to you." His voice was low and if I didn't know Rylie like I did, I would have missed the pain in his voice. "That restraining order you have is just a piece of fucking paper. It's not going to stop him. It might deter, or delay, but if he wants something from you, he's going to come for you regardless of a legal document. I still have nightmares of seeing you bruised after that hospital visit. When Katie showed me pictures, it was so hard not to go after him, because no one deserves to be beaten the way you had been. No one deserves to be treated the way Justin treated you. Give me five minutes in a dark alley." His voice had turned deadly at the end.

"Seriously?" I shook my head. "He isn't worth it, Rye."

"Luci, you mentally spiraled into those dark places in your mind because you thought I was displeased with you. When I was trying to control myself. Even with my hand on your leg, caressing you, you crawled into yourself and tried to make yourself invisible in my car, all because you *thought* I was displeased with you."

When he turned to pull my forehead to his, he said, "I don't ever want you to think you aren't good enough. So yes, I will spoil you. I will take care of you. I will allow you to live your life. But, I won't try to control you."

"A little control isn't a bad thing." I let the heat of my thoughts come through in my voice.

There was a small growl in his voice as he said, "That isn't what I mean, and you fucking know it, sweetheart."

I smiled brightly at him, and he kissed me quickly on the forehead and said, "Now let's get you upstairs so I can prove to you just how much you mean to me."

Chapter Four

My hand firmly in Rylie's, he pulled me off to a side elevator that led straight to the guest rooms, and not the general lobby. At my questioning look, he just smiled and said, "Yeah, Katie gave me the hotel information, too. I already checked you in. They didn't question it at all."

"I swear that girl." I muttered under my breath. "Just how much did you talk to her?"

"Enough to get the answers I needed."

He kissed me softly as we waited for the elevator, and when the doors opened, he practically threw my carryon into the elevator before picking me up, carrying me in, and pressing me against the wall. He kissed me fiercely as he reached over and hit one of the floor numbers. I wrapped my legs around him, and when his fingers grabbed my ass, I didn't bite back the moan that flowed through me.

He leaned back as he asked, as if we hadn't just made out like high schoolers, "You really didn't know I was meeting you at the airport? Katie didn't tell you?"

"Nope. She had just said to look to my left. That was all."

"How would she have known I was on your left? I had been pacing the length of that room for thirty minutes once I saw your plane had landed." He said, but pressed himself against me. I rolled my hips against him as he leaned forward and kissed my neck.

I tilted my head back and reveled in the feeling of his lips on my skin. It took a lot of concentration, but said, "But you know Katie. She knows things."

He hummed against my skin and when the elevator dinged and stopped, he reluctantly set me down, but not before running his hands over my bare ass and setting my dress right.

Rylie turned to grab my carryon, and when I looked at him, there was a small wet spot on the front of his pants. I huffed a chuckle, and I am sure there was a satisfied gleam in my eye.

"What?"

I reached over as the doors opened, and rubbed at it softly saying, "You may have a bit of leakage on your pants."

When I turned around, there was a couple waiting to enter. The man looked at Rylie and smiled, and the woman was laughing. I just looked at them and shrugged.

"You are horrible." Rylie said behind me after the doors closed and he took my hand again. "Come on. The room is this way."

"The last room in the hall?" I shook my head. "Let me guess. Your special request?"

"Guilty." He said, holding the door open for me, and then brazenly looked me up and down.

Soft light filled the room, and I froze when I looked at it. "This is not the room that Sam arranged for me to stay in, is it?"

"It isn't." He said, sliding his arms around my waist and kissing my neck.

I looked around at the full dresser, fifty plus inch television, king sized bed, full sitting area, and the near floor to ceiling windows with the most spectacular view of the city. Rylie reached out and pointed off to the right. Shit, there was even a lake view.

"Sam isn't going to cover this room, Rylie." I whispered the words, not knowing what to do. It was beautiful, but I was on a travel budget. The company was on a travel budget.

"Well, that is right. He will not be covering the room. I am." He whispered up my neck and nibbled on my ear.

"I'm sorry what?"

He turned me to face him, lifted my chin, so that I was looking at him. "There is much to talk about, sweetheart. Right now, though... if I don't bury myself inside of you, I might lose all semblance of sanity."

Then his lips were on mine, hands making quick work of the laces of the corset, and sliding up under my dress. His fingertips trailed lightly against my skin as he pulled my dress off in one fluid movement. I was pulling his pants off, as my bra released, and his hands were instantly there, cradling my breasts and rubbing his thumbs over my nipples.

I pulled his shirt up over his head and, before it hit the floor, he had hauled me into the air, and threw me onto the bed. When I went to sit back up, my eyes wide, the look he gave me held a command to not move a muscle. His eyes held mine as he crawled up the length of my body. His tongue swirled around one nipple and then the other as my back arched, and the movement of the butt plug hit that spot again.

"Rye." I whispered.

"Sweetheart?" His voice was smug as I moved my hips along the length of him. He pulled back and reached down, running a single finger through me, back up and around my clit, before traveling back through me and rotating the butt plug. Then he was gone.

"What are you?" I said, sitting up, and then froze when I saw him digging through my carryon. When he strode back to me, he had the lube. "Oh, fuck."

"That is the plan, sweetheart." When he reached me, he said, "On all fours."

I obeyed, but shivered when I felt the cold lube hit my skin. He worked the plug in and out, ensuring I was still plenty lubed and ready.

Only when he ran himself along the length of me, and I pushed against him, he grabbed my waist and picked me up, turning me to face him.

"What are you doing?" I said, wrapping my arms around him.

"I am not taking you the first time in weeks with your back to me." Then he spun and pressed me against the wall as he slowly lowered me onto him. Every time I had re-imagined him entering me, it paled compared to what he felt like in this moment. I felt myself constrict against him, and when he growled in my ear, I moaned. He pulled back and met my gaze. "Fuck, Luce."

"I have missed you."

He pulled out of me slowly and teased me with just the head of him. With a smirk on his face, before pushing himself back in. "You are exquisite."

"Rylie. Please." I begged, feeling every nerve in my body come alive against him.

I locked my ankles around his waist, and held on to him, as he, in slow, long, controlled movements, drew himself from me, and then pushed back in. I wasn't sure what would have been more torturous. This or if he had been pounding into me.

He rolled his hips against my clit and then pulled out one more time before slamming into me. His gray eyes still glued to mine, were filled with a heat and a meaning, I wasn't sure how to interpret.

"Cum for me, sweetheart." He said, before picking up the pace and thrusting into me deeper and deeper.

When he reached around and pushed the button on the plug, sending it vibrating through me. The effect was almost instantaneous. I fell over that cliff, clenching around his cock hard, losing all sense of awareness other than the feeling of him slamming into me relentlessly.

"Luci." He said, as he thrust one last time, and released himself into me.

We stayed there for a long moment. Still not looking away from each other. It was such a tender thing to have him stare at me the entire time he fucked me. I looked down away from him, and he said, "Don't look away. Look at me."

"But—"

"No, but's, sweetheart. You are mine, and I am yours. Don't be ashamed of what we are and what we have."

"I'm not. I'm still not used to being looked at like the way you are looking at me."

"Like you are something to hold and cherish? Like you are worthy?" He said softly, and I felt him retreating from me. "Answer me, sweetheart."

"I don't..."

He carried me to the bed, removed the plug, throwing it on the bed, and set me down. "Why? Why do you feel like I can't love you? Why I can't make love to you like this? What is it that makes you feel unworthy?"

I opened my mouth to start in on the long list of things, but he stopped me and said, "And I swear if you comment about your weight, curves, or anything that Justin put in that brain of yours, I will have only one option. That is to fuck you, silly. Well, I already plan on doing that, so... give me a real reason, Lucille Adaline Baker. One tangible real reason I can't love and adore you."

I blinked as my mind understood what he was saying and doing. "I'm sure there are some, but you are right. Old demons."

He kneeled before me, and put my face in his hands. "I will forever be trying to rid the invasive inaccurate bullshit he forced into your brain." He kissed me softly, letting me feel his love for me. "I love you so much.

That," He said with a wave toward the wall. "Was just the start, sweetheart."

He picked me back up and carried me to the bathroom, setting me on the counter. He turned the shower on and, when he was happy that the temperature was to my liking, he kissed me on the forehead and said, "Shower. I have a couple of calls to make."

I tipped my head to the side and said, "Okay."

He once again looked me up and down, and I felt his gaze settle deep in my stomach. Butterflies erupted as he bit his lip and closed the door behind him, saying, "Shower."

Chapter Five

I jumped down from the counter and stepped into the steaming water. Rinsing off quickly, I let the hot water run over me and relax my muscles. I looked to the shelf to see what there was for shampoo, and noticed that somewhere along the way, Rylie had little bottles of my favorite shampoo sitting there, waiting for me.

"You are going to spoil me rotten, Rylie James Allen."

"What was that?" He said, making me jump.

"Nothing, now let me shower."

He looked in through the glass doors, and whistled appreciatively, and when he smiled and walked out, I just shook my head.

Part of me wanted to lounge in the shower, but when I remembered he was waiting for me in the other room, I hurried to finish cleaning up. I took another second to breathe before turning the water off and grabbing a towel to dry off.

Rylie popped his head around the corner again, and then I heard him saying, "Yes... 7:00. I know it's short notice.... If we have to wait until the original time, it's fine. I just need to know... Thank you."

I towel dried my hair, and wrapped it in the towel before stepping out and seeing that he had changed into a navy-blue suit that was so dark, it was almost black.

"Rylie. What is going on?"

"We are going to dinner. Your outfit is hanging in the closet." He took a deep breath and looked me up and down and stood up off the bed.

I let my eyes trail down the length of him, and from where I was standing, appreciated how it hugged his well-defined ass. I reached up and ran my fingers along his chest, moving the jacket to the side, and let out a long breath as I noticed even the dress shirt had been tailored. It was moments like this when his breathing changed at my simple touch, that I tried to hold on to when my brain demons attacked.

Standing before me, he reached up and untucked the towel, where it fell to the floor in a heap. Rylie ran his fingertips along my skin, sending a new wave of need and pleasure through me. I hadn't realized I had closed my eyes at the feel of it until I felt his lips against my forehead.

"Let's get you dressed." He said with a heavy sigh. Heading to the closet, he retrieved a garment bag, gently laid it down on the bed, and unzipped it. "Promise not to ask too many questions."

When he pulled the dress out, I blinked.

"Did you seriously buy me a dress for dinner tonight?"

"I did." The left corner of his lip rose, and then he asked shily, "Is it okay?"

"It's beautiful." I said, running my fingers over the black, silky knit material. With spaghetti straps and v-neckline, I blinked at him. "This is a body contour dress, Rylie. It's going to show everything."

"Trust me."

"And I'm wearing this to a place that requires you to be drop dead gorgeous in a fitted suit?"

He shrugged casually. "It's just a suit. I've got a few of them back at the condo. And yes, where we are going, requires you to wear this dress." His cheeks reddened, and I reached over and gave him a quick kiss.

"There are also these." He said, holding up a pair of barely there panties and lacey strapless bra.

I raised my eyebrows, and he handed me the bra, and kneeled before me and held the panties out for me to step into, which I did. Slowly he slid them up, but when I felt his lips on my hip, I shuddered and broke out into goosebumps.

"Do you have any idea how incredibly sexy you are?" He said clasping the bra behind me. "I really rather be keeping you undressed, rather than dressing you, but you need to eat and have energy for later."

I shook my head as he turned to pull the dress off the hanger, and I fixed the bra to set it in place. Rylie undid the zipper and then held it out for me to step in. When I did, he walked around, pulling the straps up to rest on my shoulders, before he zipped it up and looped the small clasp. When I turned around, he slowly looked up the length of me and said, "I knew this would be perfect."

"You are just saying that."

He raised his eyebrows at me and pulled me over and stood behind me as we faced the floor-length mirror. The woman standing next to Rylie couldn't have been me. There was no way this dress looked this good on me.

"Still don't believe me?" He said, running his lips along my shoulder and neck, before placing a soft kiss just below my ear and snapping his eyes to mine in the mirror. That alone had me ready to push him onto the bed and ride until morning. I bit my lip as my muddy brown eyes met his in the mirror.

He visibly straightened and winked. "I have shoes too, but I know you will want to do your hair, and not leave it in a towel."

"Make up, too, if I'm supposed to be shown off." He nodded with a smirk, and I was terrified of that fact. "Rylie, this had to cost a fortune. Why am I getting the wine and dine treatment tonight? We can't afford this."

"You are worth it, and the cost isn't for you to worry about."

I studied him for a long moment, and he stood tall. "What aren't you telling me, Rylie?"

"We do have things to talk about. Our future, for one." His voice shook a little, and that alone had me fearing the answer to my next words.

"Why does that scare me?" I froze because there was only one thing that I could think of. "Rylie. If you want to break up, then do it now. I can't have a great weekend with you, only to be shattered right before I go home."

"Sweetheart. No. Stop right there." His voice was hard and demanding, but fueled by anger.

"Rylie. I ca… I can't… If this… if we're o…" I couldn't finish the sentence. It felt like my chest was caving in, and I wasn't sure if I was even breathing anymore.

His hands cradled my neck, and when he bent down to make sure that I was looking at him, tears filled my eyes at my thought, and I wasn't absorbing what he said. "No. Never. I am not going anywhere. Sweetheart, look at me. Gods, please look at me and listen."

I blinked over and over again, feeling tears fall onto my cheeks, and I thought I heard him whisper something that sounded like, "I would be nothing without you by my side. Don't second guess us."

I met his gaze, and he kissed me softly. "I am not going anywhere. Breathe. I. Am. Right. Here."

After a couple of minutes, where he just stood there, running his thumbs across my cheekbones, he said, "I know you are scared. Breathe, my love."

Another minute went by, and I reached up where his hands were on my neck and squeezed on his hand as I nodded.

"Okay." I said, shame now filling me. "I'm sorry, Rye."

"No reason to apologize." He kissed my forehead quickly, and I could feel the tension in his hands as he rested his forehead on mine and said, "I'm not mad. I know that he would be raging right now, but I'm not him. I won't—"

"Rylie. I know you are not Justin." I took a deep breath.

"Good. I'd never degrade you like that. You are the sun in the darkness, Sweetheart." He sighed heavily, and his voice shook as he whispered, "I promise to prove it to you this weekend."

What? Did he just say prove? He has nothing to prove. Gods, I had to pull myself together. Why was I second guessing this so much? Something was different about this trip, and I couldn't fully figure out what was going on. I took a big deep breath and let it out, counting to ten as my therapist had taught me.

I looked at the clock and I asked, "How long does it take to get to the restaurant? You said we have a 7:00pm reservation, right?"

"They will hold the table all night. We go when you are ready." His eyes searched mine.

"What?"

"Are you okay?"

I took a deep breath. "Yeah. I'm good."

"Are *we* good?" There was a touch of fear in his voice as I reached up and put my hand on his cheek.

"Yeah. I'm good if you are."

He nodded.

"Then I'm going to go get my hair and makeup done so I don't waste this dress and dinner you apparently have planned."

When I turned into the bathroom, I looked back at where Rylie was standing. He was running both hands through his hair, head tipped back, staring at the ceiling. I took one last long breath before stepping into the bathroom to finish getting ready.

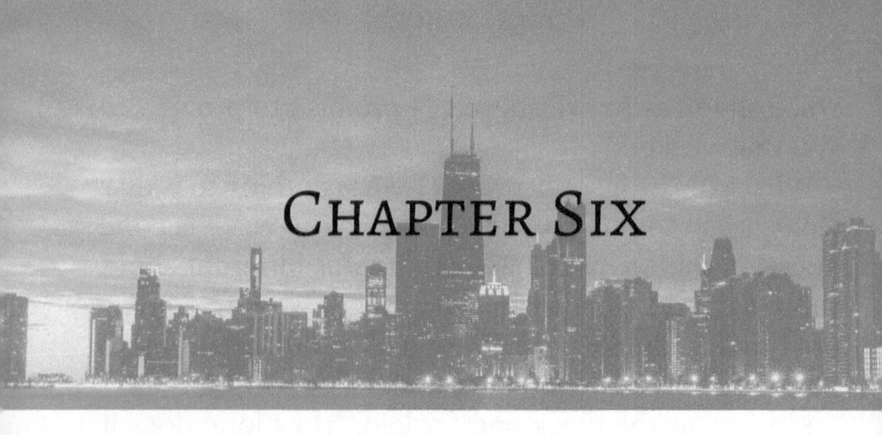

Chapter Six

Rylie was just getting into the car when my phone started pinging repeatedly. I pulled it out and shook my head.

Katie the PIMA BFF:
Like your surprise?
Come on, answer me.
I know you are with him.
God. Will you two stop fucking for just a moment so I can talk to you?

Luci:
Just got in the car to go to dinner, bitch.
Yes, I liked the surprise.
A little warning next time would be nice.
How do you know these things?

Katie the PIMA BFF:
It's what I do.

Luci:
Seriously though.
Why didn't you tell me you gave him the flight info?

Katie the PIMA BFF:

Because you would be pissed at me.

> **Luci:**
> **He needed to sleep, Katie.**
> **I had my reasons.**

Katie the PIMA BFF:
Your reasons are stupid.

> **Luci:**
> **You're stupid.**

Katie the PIMA BFF:
We aren't five. Use your words.

> **Luci:**
> **:P**

"Who are you texting?" Rylie asked when we got to the light. He reached over and laid his hand on my thigh. It felt a little clammy, and his index bounced like when he was nervous. I looked over at him, narrowing my eyes slightly, but he just gave me a small reassuring smile.

"Katie." I shook my head. "Just giving her shit about telling you the flight info."

"She did fight me on it."

"I'm not sure if that makes me feel better or worse."

Katie the PIMA BFF:
Just remember you love me.
Most of all. Just remember you love Rylie.

> **Luci:**
> **What does that even mean?**

Katie the PIMA BFF:
Just remember this is the Rylie you've known forever, and love him just the way he is.

> **Luci:**
> **Can you not be vague for one minute of your life?**

Katie the PIMA BFF:
Promise me you will remember that.

Luci:
What the fuck, Katie?

Katie the PIMA BFF:
Luci?

Luci:
Fine. It's an easy promise to give.
You know I love him with every ounce of breath in me.
You, on the other hand...

Katie the PIMA BFF:
Good. I got a hot date tonight, and so do you.
Ha! You love me. Don't even try to deny it.
I'll catch you in a few days, okay?
Call me if you need rescuing.

Luci:
Okay. Love you, bitch.

Katie the PIMA BFF:
Love you more.

As Rylie pulled up to the restaurant, it was sprinkling, and I was grateful for the covered entrance. I had gone with a full face of makeup and my brown hair was pulled half up, with small ringlets falling to the front. When he got out of the car, I heard the valet say, "Good evening, Mr. Allen."

I blinked, because I had never heard anyone call him Mr. Allen before. Rylie was at my door, reaching for my hand to help me out. When I was out of the car, Rylie instantly had his hand at my back, guiding me forward. There was a lot of media outside, and flashes of light came from all directions.

"What is going on, Rylie?"

I didn't look at him, but he bent down to whisper in my ear, "It's a popular restaurant for bigwigs, so they hang out and just take photos, hoping to catch the next news story."

There was something in his voice that left me guarded, but when we got inside, he slid his jacket off, and held it as the host glanced up, and said, "This way, Mr. Allen."

My phone vibrated repeatedly again, and I silently cursed Katie. I pulled it out as we made our way to the table.

Sam:
We need to video chat now.

Luci:
I'm at dinner. Can we talk later?

Sam:
This isn't something that can wait.
Consider it an emergency.

When we reached the table, I turned to Rylie, rolled my eyes, and said, "I need to video chat with Sam for a few minutes. There is apparently a crisis of some sort that he can't handle long enough for me to have dinner with you."

Rylie turned to the host and asked, "Is there somewhere private she can take a call?"

"Of course, Mr. Allen." He turned to me, and said, "This way, Miss."

"I'm sorry, Rylie."

"It's okay, sweetheart." There was a heat in his voice, as his eyes looked me up and down as he said, "Hurry back."

"Of course." I turned to leave, but he grabbed my hand, pulling me back to him, and with his other hand, pulled my head up for a quick kiss.

I pulled back slightly, noting my lipstick on his lips. I reached up and wiped it off, but he smirked, as I said, "Aren't you worried about others seeing us together?"

"We wouldn't have left the hotel if I cared if people saw us together. I wouldn't have bought that dress for you. I wouldn't have brought you here. So, no. I don't care." Then his voice deepened in that way, that made my toes curl. "Let everyone see that you are mine, sweetheart."

I smiled then and felt a little guilty for the freakout I had earlier. While I didn't understand much of what he had just said, I turned to follow the host down the hall near the kitchens. My phone vibrated non-stop all the way to the small room. "You'll have your privacy in here, ma'am."

"Thank you, sir."

"Anything for you and Mr. Allen." He said, bowing slightly, and I watched him leave in confusion. I turned and there was sound tiles on the walls, which created a calming wave pattern across the gray walls. My heels sunk into the dark gray carpet as I sat down at the desk on the far wall. My phone vibrated again, and I sighed.

I went to my contacts, and just video called Sam without looking at the messages. When he answered, he looked serious.

"Mind telling me what is such a 911 that I couldn't have dinner first?" I snapped. I was hungry, tired, and horny. Three things that did not mix well in Luci Baker.

"Mind telling me why I got six, no seven, text messages that you are out, dressed to the nines with Rylie Allen?"

I looked at him in confusion. "I don't think I need to answer that. One, it has nothing to do with work. Two, I'm not on the clock right now. Besides, what does one have to do with the other?"

"We will circle back around to that." He ran his hand through his hair and pulled at his tie, undoing it and throwing it off to the side. He looked off camera, as I heard a bunch of coughing, and I remembered his daughter was sick.

"How's your baby girl?"

"Helen just got home, so she's attending to her."

"Okay, so again, what is the emergency?"

"Short version. I realize that we just started jumping from Chicago and Houston recently, but there has been a change in plans."

I eyed him carefully, and when he didn't say anything, I said, "I'm waiting."

"The clients in Chicago want more hands-on, in person attention."

"So, are you assigning the account to a local person? No more trips to Chicago? I don't understand why you called this a 911 call. We could have discussed this in the morning, or I don't know, after I ate dinner at least." I sat back in the chair and crossed my arms tight.

"No, Luci, this couldn't wait. What I'm doing is offering you an opportunity to move to Chicago to work mainly on the Henderson Account. You will still be responsible for the Mann and Wright accounts in Houston, but the Henderson accounts will be more demanding. They like you, and want to continue working with you, but they demand more in person interaction."

"So, you want me to pick up and move my life to Chicago for an account that we still don't know will be long term?"

"I spoke to Ray Henderson this evening. He said that if we agree to the terms he set forth tonight, one of which is a personal rep here in Chicago, preferably one specific Luci Baker, then he will sign a ten-year contract, with an automatic ten-year renewal provision, if the deadlines are met." He looked at me again after tipping his head back and sighing. "The firm will also increase your pay by $40,000 a year, you keep all your current benefits, the firm will pay all moving expenses, first six months of housing, and an additional week of vacation for you to agree to the position."

I blinked. That... That was some incentive.

"Think about it, but I need an answer in the morning." Sam said.

"Sam, that..." My heart was racing. I looked off through the wall to where I thought Rylie was sitting and blinked a few times.

"I know it's a lot. You just got settled in San Jose. I know how hard the last few years have been."

"And you have to know before the meeting tomorrow?"

Sam nodded. "Mr. Henderson is arriving at ten, so we need to know how to move forward."

"Alright, fine. I'll let you know when I arrive in the morning." Shaking my head in disbelief, I noticed his eyes go to something just off camera. "I understand the offer is time sensitive, but you keep refusing to tell me why this is a 911, Sam."

"Because now I have fifteen text messages, asking me why you are out with Rylie Allen. Care to tell me why?" Sam said and smiled.

"Once again, that is none of your business." I sighed. "How do you even know who Rylie is?"

"How do I even know who...?" Sam stuttered. "Do *you* know who Rylie Allen is?"

A frustrated groan slipped out as I fought the urge to hang up on him. "I've known him for half my life. He's one of the most important people in my existence, so yes, I know exactly who Rylie Allen is. Now if you don't mind, I am going to go back to having dinner, because I am starved." Sam's eyes were huge as I said, "I'll see you in the morning with my answer."

Chapter Seven

After ending the call, I just stared at the wall for a long moment before my stomach growled. I stood and when I walked out into the main dining area, my eyes went directly to Rylie's, whose rose and met mine. The smile on his face was dazzling.

I strode right for him, and when I reached the table, he was already standing and holding the seat out for me. "You really are going to spoil me this trip, aren't you?"

He shrugged. "You deserve it."

"But when you are back home, we don't do… well, this." I said, waving my hand to encompass all that was around us. Black suits, fancy dresses, and the glass of red that likely cost more than the pair of running shoes I had back at the hotel per glass. "Fuck, Rylie, the last few times we were here, we hardly left the hotel, not that I'm complaining about that."

"Back home, I'm just Rylie. We go to the lake, fish, camp, and do normal things. We hang out with our mutual friends, and things are… simpler."

"Yet, here you are somehow, Mr. Allen." I eyed him, and he was fidgeting with his glass, causing the red liquid to swirl. "Rylie. You said we need to talk, and we really do for a multitude of reasons. One of which is why my boss, who just offered me the position of a lifetime, which I won't tell you about because my decision could be affected by what you are holding out, asked why I was out with you tonight."

Rylie looked at me and blinked. "Care to repeat that slower next time?"

"My boss, just called to offer me a position of a lifetime. Before I tell you what that is, I want to know why he was curious why I was out to dinner with my boyfriend, not that he knows that is who you are to me."

"What did you tell him?" His voice was low, and he was studying his glass again. There was something in the way he wouldn't make eye contact with me that worried me.

"What did I tell him when he asked why I was out with Rylie Allen? I told him it wasn't any of his fucking business. Professionally, of course, but the point was made." I reached over and made Rylie look at me. "Now, tell me who you are."

"You know who I am. The rest is bullshit and image." He said, taking my hand in his. His eyes focused on our joined hands before he said, "None of that matters. None of the bullshit matters when you are by my side, and *you* know the real me."

"Rylie." I drew out his name and gave him a look. "What have you been hiding from me?"

He turned my hand and kissed my palm. "I didn't want to tell you like this. I had a plan for this weekend. For everything. This is not how I had planned it. Promise me you won't look at me differently."

"I promise." That was pure worry in his eyes. No, fear. He was terrified that whatever he was going to tell me was going to change us.

"After Shannon and I separated, I needed a new start. As you know, I met Harper when I moved here, and as you also know, he helped me get my feet on the ground. He did more than that, actually. He silently made me a partner in his business." His eyes flicked up to me and I realized what he was telling me.

"Harper made you a partner in Webster Enterprises?" I blinked. Repeatedly. Webster Enterprises was the number one tech development firm in the US.

"Full partner." He breathed. "Just he and I."

"Harper died a year ago." I looked around and realization hit.

"He did, and there isn't a day that goes by that I don't miss him terribly." I stared at him. "When the trust and final will were read, I inherited the entire company. All tech rights, all copyrights, all trademarks, all things Webster Enterprises. Everything. Much to the Board of Directors' chagrin."

Rylie and I had only been together for about six months at the time Harper had died, and he had flown me out for the funeral. There had been a lot of sideways looks at Rylie, but it hadn't mattered. Harper was our friend, and we were there to mourn him.

Our dinner came, and it smelled divine, but I just watched Rylie. "I ordered while you were on the phone. I hope it's okay."

I sat there, totally and completely stunned. I had assumed the company had been passed on down to Harper's nieces and nephews, but Rylie? Rylie got everything?

"Sweetheart, please say something."

"Holy fucking shit, Rye!" I said it a tad too loud, and the silence that came from the neighboring tables made him chuckle.

"Well, that's one way to respond to finding out that you are madly in love with a billionaire."

"I'm sorry, what?" I asked, as I glanced around, because everything pointed to this being the truth. The fancy clothes, dinner, new car...

"Are you going to tell me you aren't?" He smirked and then he bit his bottom lip, making that very predominate pulsing happen between my legs again, because fuck if that look wasn't sexy as hell...

"Why didn't you tell me? Did you not trust me? Did you think I would only stay with you for the money?" I asked because well it hurt that he hadn't told me. He knew everything about me. He knew me better than I knew myself.

"I knew it didn't matter to you. I knew you loved me for me. I can just be Rylie with you. I never have to be Mr. Allen or the sole heir to Webster Enterprises. I am just Rylie. There was this part of me that thought you wouldn't want me anymore, and..." The look in his eyes broke my heart. "I just want to be Rylie with you."

I nodded. Strangely, I understood that. "So it isn't that you thought I would want you for your money?"

He huffed a laugh. "Any other relationship I've had? Shannon? I would say yes. You, though, Luci? No. Not with you. I've never once thought you would want me for my money."

I leaned back, crossed my arms, and stared him down. "So, tell me, why would you think I wouldn't want to be with you now?"

"The publicity is a lot." He said, looking out the window to the line of photographers out front. "I know how hard you have worked to hide from Justin. If you are with me, he will find out. The whole world will find out."

"How is it that I never heard that you... wait... you were worried I wouldn't want to be with you anymore because Justin would find out?" Now I was pissed. I stood up, and stood before him. He looked up at me, and I pushed his chair back and sat in his lap. His arms circled around my waist, and I said, "You are such a stupid fucking idiot, Rye."

I kissed him with everything I had. I fed every feeling I had for him into that kiss. When he opened for me, he moaned and I felt him harden under my lap. Our tongues danced, and I breathed him in. No matter what he was right, he was still my Rylie. I pulled back, breathless. "Don't you ever fucking doubt me again, asshole."

"You know that the second you kissed me, every camera in this place went off, right?" His words were a whisper against my lips that I felt turn up slightly.

"Can I be a public bitch for a minute?" I cooed and his eyes met mine.

"I don't like that glint in your eye, sweetheart." He just reached out and kissed me again. "You are going to be a public relations nightmare, aren't you?"

"Rylie. I love you. If you want me to behave, I will. At least I'll try to behave, but you know I have a mouth. If anyone says something that I don't agree with, I'm going to say something." I got up off his lap, swaying my hips a bit more than necessary as I sat back down before my dinner.

"The media is actually being very well behaved considering that this is the first time they have seen me with a woman since..."

"Since you became Mr. Rylie Allen?" He nodded. "Okay. I'll behave. Though I suspect that kiss will be on every front-page media outlet by morning?"

He smiled and said, "It will. Now will you please eat? I know you are hungry." I raised an eyebrow at him, and he mirrored the movement, before his voice dropped and he said, "Eat, sweetheart."

I couldn't help the satisfaction in getting him to be more forceful with his words and started eating.

I really didn't care about Rylie's money. He was right in that I loved him for him. Justin had been from a well-off family, and look how he had been. An A-Class asshole. So no, Rylie's money didn't matter to me. It wasn't like it was mine. It's his. I did have the passing thought that maybe he would tire of me and get himself a trophy wife, but I huffed a laugh, shaking my head at myself.

Rylie's voice pulled me from my thoughts. "What?"

"Just had a passing thought that maybe you would leave me for a trophy wife."

His eyebrows shot to the ceiling, then his gaze flicked over me. "You fit the appearance of one, but what you bring to the table is so much more than those brainless, cackling hens. I hate having to attend events and seeing all those women just bitching because they didn't have whatever it was that released that week, earlier than someone else. It's all bullshit, Luce. It really is."

"Will you want me to..." I trailed off.

"Sweetheart, I am not going to have you do anything you don't want to do. Personally, I would like to keep you away from those women for as long as possible. It's one of the many reasons I didn't tell you. You would hate every minute of it, or as I said earlier, you would be a PR nightmare."

I popped a piece of steak in my mouth, chewing as I kept my eye on him, and when he gave me a look like, 'Well?'

"If you want me to stay around, I'll be a nightmare. You know I can't keep my mouth shut."

He hummed at that and said, "But I like what your mouth can do when it's open."

"You just wait, Mr. Allen. I'll show you *exactly* what it can do."

"I'll hold you to that. But first I want to see it eating some food, because you aren't eating."

I conceded, because the steak was delicious, and popped another bite in my mouth.

THE REST OF THE dinner was pretty uneventful. There were still some turned heads and hushed whispers as people passed, but otherwise, it was just like any other dinner out with Rylie. He dug his spoon into the chocolate lava cake, scooped a little of the vanilla-caramel ice cream, and lifted it to my mouth, cupping his hand underneath.

I smirked at him. "You are enjoying this aren't you?"

"What? Treating you like the princess you are?" His voice was a little deeper than the situation called for, and I narrowed my eyes at him. He answered by lifting the spoon a bit more, and I leaned forward to take the bite. "Damn straight I am."

A few minutes later, when the plate was all but licked clean and Rylie and I were talking about Katie's new boyfriend, the manager said, "Mr. Allen. Ma'am." He nodded quickly and turned back toward Rylie. "Mr. Allen, we cleared out most of the media out front. We will pull your car around when you are ready."

Rylie's eyes met mine, and he raised an eyebrow. I nodded, and he turned to the manager and said, "Thank you, Raul. I believe we are ready to leave."

"Very well, sir. I'll have your car brought out front."

"Is it always like this?" I asked with a small smirk.

"Like what?"

"Yes, sir. No, sir. We will wipe your ass for you, Mr. Allen." I chuckled softly, because I knew it probably bothered him on a personal level. He confirmed it with the twitch in his jaw. I sighed lightly, "You tolerate it because of the image."

"Yeah. It has taken a hot minute to get used to."

"So, what you are saying is that I'm going to need to be a quick study, and at least *try* not to be a PR nightmare?"

I smiled at him knowingly, and he just shook his head before saying, "Let's go, Luce."

He stood, and I took his outstretched hand. There were still a few people outside trying to remove reporters. Most had been moved across the street. I glanced at them, and froze when my eyes landed on a tall brown-haired man. He wasn't holding a camera, but instead just stood there in a black jacket with his hands in his pockets.

Rylie's arm tugged on mine, but I couldn't move. My feet might as well have been nailed to the concrete. All I saw was Justin striding for me.

The man stopped and smirked as my vision faded back to that old apartment in Sacramento, where Justin cornered me in the living room. Saw Justin coming at me, fists balled up, and hissing through his teeth how I had disappointed him by not having dinner ready when he got home.

There were small quick movements on my cheeks, and I tried to pull back, but I couldn't move.

"Lucille." Rylie.

That was Rylie's voice. I concentrated on that voice, and when my vision cleared, his gray eyes were locked onto mine, studying me.

"Rylie." His name came out as a mixture of a relieved sigh and a desperate plea. I wrapped my arms around his waist. I vaguely heard the shuttering of the cameras, and buried my face further into his chest as he held me close. There were voices shouting for the media to leave, and I lifted my head and looked around Rylie's shoulder. The man was gone.

It couldn't have been Justin. Right? There was no way he could know I was in Chicago right now.

"Luce." Rylie's finger and thumb pinched my chin, bringing my face around to look at him. I blinked again and let the sound of his voice flow over me.

"Rylie." I breathed again, letting my breath out slowly. "I'm sorry. I thought..." I swallowed hard and took a deep breath to let my breath flow freely again. "I thought I saw Justin. I'm so sorry."

His head whipped around as he pulled me back into his arms. He scanned the area and held me until his car pulled up. Rylie held me tight as he guided me to the passenger seat. I'm not sure if he opened the door or if the valet did, but I felt him nod to someone and then kissed me quickly on my temple before stepping back and closing the door.

There was no way that Justin could be here. How would he know? No one from the office would have told him where I was. The entire firm knew what Justin had done that night. Sam had even paid to have the restraining order put in place. He had even taken it upon himself to walk me to and from my car every day until I was comfortable enough to do it alone. It was one reason we all worked remotely now.

I jumped slightly when the driver's side door opened and Rylie slid into the seat. He reached over, grabbed my hand, and threaded his fingers through mine. He squeezed tightly and let out a long, slow breath. "How about we go for a walk to help clear your head? There's this place I know and wanted to show you. I promise it's quiet."

I couldn't speak, and so I nodded.

"Luce?" He pulled my face toward his and kissed me softly, letting his lips linger. I lifted my other hand and cradled his cheek. Fuck it. Let the world see Rylie was mine. No one could calm me from the horrors like Rylie could. No one could make me feel like I actually mattered more than Rylie. He was my everything, and regardless of all that had happened tonight, and how much my world was going to change, I had Rylie. That was all that mattered.

"Yeah?" I whispered against his lips.

"I love you."

I smiled brightly at that, letting those words wash away the tension that had flooded my body.

"I love you, too."

Chapter Eight

We drove through the city, rain drops streaking across the window, my mind went back to that phone call with Sam. My thoughts swirled around that $40,000 a year salary increase. They could hire a grad for that. Why me, though? I thought through all the elements of the project and I could see why they would want the personal rep, but would it be wise to move to Chicago? Would Rylie even want me in Chicago? There were so many thoughts going through my head that I hadn't realized Rylie had parked until he pinched my chin between his finger and thumb, and made me look at him.

"Where did you go, sweetheart?"

"Just thinking." He gave me a questioning look, and I shook my head.

"We will talk about it later." I pointed out of the car. "It's raining, and while I don't mind getting wet, was there something specific you wanted to show me? Or are we just going to sit here? Where is here, anyway?"

"Lincoln Park, well a secluded portion of Lincoln Park. This time of night, it's pretty quiet." There was a wicked glint in his eye. "Here, put these flats on. It will be easier to walk. While it's selfish of me to have you wear heels because they make your legs and ass look fantastic, I know it will be easier for you to walk."

"I'll remember that for later." I opened the door before he could say anything else, and stepped out into the rain. It was warmer than what I was used to, and the drops hitting my skin instantly soothed away some of the previous anxiety and tension. I tilted my face up and let them fall, picturing them literally washing my cares away.

"How do you do it?"

"Do what?" I asked, genuinely confused. I was still relishing in the feel of the heavy drops as they plunked onto my face, arms, chest before he came to stand before me, wrapping his arms around my waist pulling me to him.

"Make being so beautiful effortless. Inside and out."

"I really don't know what you are talking about. Come on, show me what you wanted to show me." I pulled away, turned, and ran down the path, and had just made it onto a landing when I threw my arms out wide and twirled and danced in the rain for a moment. I heard his feet hit the wet planks, and there was only a small pause before he wrapped his arms back around my waist, picked me up, and swung me around in circles.

Laughter bubbled up and burst through my lips. He set me down, and I turned to face him. The small lapping of water against the landing was soothing, and swore I heard geese flapping in the water. Back home I would have been hesitant to be out in the middle of a large park, but with Rylie, I always felt safe.

I looked up at him, and there was maybe three inches between us. I didn't know how long we stood there just staring into each other's eyes, but at one point he reached up and moved some of the drenched hair away from my eyes. It was raining hard now, and I was soaked to the bone. It was the strangest sensation to not be cold in the rain. Rylie's eyes were full of wonder, and I couldn't help but smile at the man before me.

"This. This is why I love you so much." I tilted my head to the side in question, and he continued, "We can just be us here. We can just love each other for who we are."

I stepped back, unsure of what he was saying, and he grabbed my hips to hold me to him. I felt him harden against me, and I ran my fingers along the waistband of his pants, tugging slightly. When I pulled back, and reached down to run a finger along his full length, there was a needy moan that came from him. "Can you blame me? I've been hard since you sat on my lap at the restaurant. This is what you do to me."

"Humm. If it's my fault, I should probably fix it then, huh?" I kissed him as I unbuckled his belt and loosened his pants. "I believe you said something about holding me to showing you what my mouth could do?"

I dropped to my knees and released him through the zipper, licking the tip. The salty taste of him on my lips made that spot deep in my stomach tighten, and his hand was gentle on the side of my head as I took him further into my mouth and bobbed up and down.

A bright light flashed across us and he pulled me up and close to his chest, just as an officer made their way over. A giggle burst from my lips as I tried to discreetly put him away.

"The park is closed."

"Yes, sir. Sorry. My girl is from out of town, and wanted to dance in the Midwest rain. No better place than the park." Rylie said. I was chuckling, and he slapped my ass.

"That won't fool him." I whispered.

"Shut up." He tried not to laugh, but there was a little snort that emanated from him.

When the officer reached us, we had already put ourselves back together, and so I turned to face him. The light flashed in my face, and I winced. When the light hit Rylie's face, the officer's 'Oh shit.' was quiet but audible.

"I'm sorry, Mr. Allen." He said when he composed himself. "I didn't realize."

I looked up at Rylie, who trying not to laugh, and slid his hand up the back of my dress, resting his hand on my ass. I wasn't going to lie. The risk of being caught was invigorating. My nipples hardened, and I shifted my weight, feeling myself slick in excitement.

"I will leave you two to your evening." The officer said, then turned and jogged off.

"You lucky bastard." I said, thumping his chest once the officer was out of earshot.

"It is a perk. It isn't fair, but it's better than having the press to deal with, not to mention my team of lawyers. I'd rather not have to explain why I got caught getting head from the most beautiful woman on the planet in the middle of a very public park. That is not on my list of things to do this weekend, sweetheart."

I turned back down the walkway, and after sauntering a few steps away, I looked over my shoulder to see Rylie holding his fist in his mouth. I smirked and cooed, "Back to the hotel then, so I can finish what I started?"

CHAPTER NINE

Rylie fumbled with the unlocking mechanism of our hotel suite before finally opening the door. I pulled his belt off and threw it behind us into the hallway as he chuckled, and when he pulled me into the room, I smirked at him. Leaving a string of wet clothes from the door to the bed, I pushed him against the wall, where I dropped back to my knees and wrapped my hand around the base of his cock, stroking and sucking.

When I took him all the way down my throat, all I heard was a breathy, "Fuck, Luci." I hummed into him, and he lifted me up and off him. A disappointed whine came out, causing him to smile. "Sweetheart, if I don't get inside you, I'm going to be very grumpy."

I kissed him, and then whispered teasingly, "Well, I wouldn't want Mr. Allen grumpy."

Rylie had me against the wall before I could take a breath. His hand threaded tight in my hair, and the other on my hips, securing me in place. He leaned down and whispered against my jaw, making my whole body break out in goosebumps. "Let me make something extraordinarily clear, sweetheart. I will *never* be Mr. Allen with you."

"I know, but it was fun to tease you with." I said, but noticed the look in his eyes. "It bothers you that much?"

He carried me to the edge of the bed, kneeled before me, and ran his fingers along the anklet he gave me at Christmas. "I am just Rylie with you, please."

"Is that what you are scared of? Of me finding out that you are Mr. Allen, and have it change how I see you." I blinked in full realization that this was a very real fear of his.

His throat bobbed, and the grip on my foot tightened. He studied me for a long moment before his hand loosened just slightly as it ran up and wrapped around the anklet. "When I gave you this." He gave me a soft kiss on the nose before he said, "It was a symbol of my dedication to you and only you. I promised to take care of you. To ensure that all your needs were met. Protect you in any way I can. You are my everything, and to have you look at me or treat me like Mr. Allen. I can't bear that, Luce."

"Oh, Rylie." My heart broke for him. "My feelings for you have not changed one damn bit. If anything, the fact that you are still you, even after all this has happened to you, makes me love you all the more."

One moment he was studying me with such intensity that I couldn't help but squirm, and the next, his lips were crashing onto mine. When I resisted, he picked my hips up, and threw me up onto the bed.

"Luci..." His voice was full of that dominance that instantly made me wetter and ready for him. I could only give him a whined moan in response as I gave into his control.

"That's my good girl." He said, crawling up the bed to meet me.

I was half sitting up, and as he kneeled over me, he reached down, ran a thumb over my lips that I caught between my teeth, sucked, and ran my tongue along the tip. A purely devilish grin crossed his lips as his eyes trailed down my body. Then his fingers were sliding between the folds between my legs.

Two fingers teased the opening, but his eyes dragged up to me. When they met mine, they burrowed deep within me. "Who do you belong to, Luce?"

The question made my heart jump, then swell, as his fingers found that spot along the front wall, making me bow my back toward him. A loud moan was pulled from my lips as he repeated the motion.

"Sweetheart, answer me."

"Hum?" I asked, not remembering what he had said. I was flying in the clouds. Rylie had always been able to bring me so much pleasure.

A low chuckle came from him as he withdrew his fingers from me and licked his fingers clean, his eyes not leaving mine. When he was done, he said, "Who do you belong to, sweetheart?"

"You, Rylie. Only you." I panted.

"Yeah, you do." He moaned as he thrust into me in a single stroke.

"Oh, fuck me!" I said under my breath.

Rylie chuckled and grabbed ahold of my ankles, spreading them wide to the side as he did just that.

Moments later, I was begging Rylie to let me cum. He reached down and flicked my clit, and I whimpered loudly. "Rye."

"Cum for me, sweetheart." He pressed on my clit again, and when I lost control, he pounded into me hard and fast, extending out my pleasure. He slowed as I came down and bent down to kiss me. Rylie lifted me to sit and moved one of the pillows and patted it.

I smirked at him, laid with my ass toward him, and my chest on the pillow he laid out. I felt the cool liquid run down the center of me, across my ass, and through my already wet pussy. His finger massaged and circled the rosebud before slowly entering me. In and out, before a second followed suit.

I pushed back against him as the head of his cock rubbed against my clit. I bit my lip and moaned. A small huffed chuckle from Rylie behind me, had me saying, "Are you just going to sit here and tease me, Rylie? Or are you going to fuck my ass like you have been wanting to all night?"

His fingers were gone, and then there was a smack that rang through the air, that was quickly followed by stinging heat and my moan. Another smack, and I felt myself quiver.

His hand rested on the small of my back. Rylie teased me by rubbing himself up and down me, before pressing against my ass. I groaned impatiently as the head of his cock popped in and then moving in a little further before Rylie started thrusting in short small strokes.

"God, Rylie."

Slowly, he pushed into me more, and I bit down on the pillow to keep from screaming in pleasure. When he was fully within me, Rylie paused, ran his hand up my back, to wrap around my neck as he bent down and kissed my shoulder. He pulled me up, turning my head to face him, and kissed me as he pulled out an inch and then back in, slowly, gently.

I bit his bottom lip, and when he pulled out this time, he slammed into me with a force that took all the air out of my lungs. His other hand reached around and circled my clit, but there was something else in his hand, too. He slammed back into me and held me against him. One hand on my neck, the other between my legs, inserting a dildo into me. "I know it's not the real thing, yet."

"You know I want to explore. You also know how much I love having your cock and a dildo filling me, so—" My words were cut off as he turned the vibrator on, and a loud moan filled the room. "Oh fuck, Rye."

"One day, sweetheart, but tonight, you are mine."

"Then fuck my ass and make me cum." Smiling over my shoulder, he bent me over and pounded into me. I met him stroke for stroke, feeling myself getting closer.

I looked over my shoulder, where he gave me a small nod. Reaching down and fingering my clit, he picked up the pace. I couldn't help the screams that came from my throat. Only Rylie. Only Rylie could make me feel like this. Only he could... I shattered. I lost every thought in my head as my muscles gripped him hard and he thrust in one last time, releasing himself deep within me.

He pulled me up, turned my head toward him again and kissed me. We collapsed onto the bed, and the dildo slid out from me.

"I don't know if I can let you go home, Luci." He kissed the spot where my neck and shoulder met. "I'm addicted to you, and..."

"And what, Rye?" I turned to face him and there was something in his eyes I couldn't place.

"I love you." He moved some stray hair from my face and tucked it behind my ear. I smiled at him before he gave me a quick kiss and pulled me in tighter. "Get some sleep."

Chapter Ten

I woke up curled up against Rylie holding me tight against him. Shifting and he tugged me closer and whispered my name. I cherished the feel of him against me, and how, even in sleep, he wanted me close. God, I never wanted to leave his side again and to wake every morning in his arms.

So much was changing on this trip, though. But Rylie was still Rylie. I sighed, content in that thought, and rested my hand over his, running my thumb back and forth across his knuckles as I thought through dinner last night. It started with that damn job offer that was then complicated by Rylie telling me he was the freaking heir to Webster Enterprises. He was right, though. What did it change between us?

Nothing. It just meant he had a demanding job that could provide for him and his family. So the only thing that this revelation meant was that any time we were in public, it would indeed be public. There would be no hiding from the media.

I let out a long breath in confusion as I wondered how I had not found out. Was my head so deep into my work and talking to Rylie that I never paid any attention to the major player turnovers? Sure, there had been discussion about Webster Enterprises at work. There would be, considering they were such a big deal, but I hadn't heard a whisper of who was at the helm. I knew that they had been friends, but I never would have dreamed that Harper would have turned everything over to Rylie.

He had been temperamental during that time, but I thought it was from the loss of his best friend. He would always seem to be better by the time we finished seeing each other. In reality, it was the loss of his friend and the stress of taking over a new billion-dollar company. I smiled as pride swelled within me. Rylie had helped it to continue to grow and flourish in the last year.

My phone went off, and I reached over and looked at it. Rylie pulled me back to him when I snuggled back up next to him.

Sam:
Decision?

Luci:
I'll have my decision for you at 9.

Sam:
Luci.

Luci:
See you at 9.

"Why is someone texting this early in the fucking morning?" Rylie said, burying his head deeper into my hair. "Don't tell me it's someone from home, because we both know it's too early for our friends, too. God, it has to be, what, three in the morning there?"

"Just Sam." I turned to face Rylie. "He wants my decision."

"Want to talk it out?" He said, kissing my forehead. "And good morning, sweetheart."

"Good morning. Morning breath or not. I'm getting a good morning kiss." I brought my hand up and cupped his cheek as I kissed him.

He pushed up against me, and I felt him hard against my leg. "I can give you more than a kiss."

I smirked and wrapped a leg around his hip. "I need to decide about work."

"You don't have to work. I can more than provide for us. But it is your decision. I don't think you could *not* work, actually. Talk it out. Use me as sounding board." He was rambling, and when my eyes met his, my heart pounded in my chest.

"It would, well, could change things, even more for us." I looked down and fingered the grooves in his chest.

Rylie went very still. "How much?"

My voice shook as I said, "He offered me a raise of $40,000 a year to be the personal rep for one of the accounts."

His eyes went wide with that. "They could hire someone for that. Train them to be your assistant."

I nodded. "That's what I said."

"What else?"

"It would mean more in-person meetings. So many more that they are offering to pay my moving expenses and to pay six months of housing costs for me to take the position."

"And where is this account?" His hands hadn't moved from my hips, and I didn't know if Rylie was even breathing. I met his gaze, and I didn't know why I held back, but maybe I was scared. What if Rylie didn't want me here?

Wait, did he just say that I didn't need to work? That he would provide for both of us? I shook my head and stared at him.

"What do you mean, you could provide for both of us?"

"Just what I said. If you don't take the promotion, I'm assuming you will either be released due to job duty necessity or reassigned. I would happily take care of you. You know that."

I blinked. "You would?"

"You are mine, Lucille Adaline Baker. Do you really think I would leave you to fend for yourself?" He sighed, "But you are avoiding a pretty important question."

I ran my hand down his chest and let my hand rest over his heart. It was pounding, and I saw his chest shudder at the touch.

"Luci, please. Where?"

"Here." I said, lifting my eyes to meet his.

"I'm sorry. Did you just say here?"

I nodded. "The position would be here in Chicago."

The next thing I knew, he was lying on top of me and kissing me. He pulled back and said, "Please tell me you aren't fucking with me right now?"

"I'm not. The job is here in Chicago."

"That fixes so many problems." He said, kissing me again.

"How?" I asked when he finally stopped covering my face in kisses. "If I take this job, there will be a higher media presence on you than before, because we will have to go out into public even more. We can't just hide away forever. We both have jobs to do. Then there is the hassle of packing, finding a new place to live out here... God, I hate house and apartment hunting."

"What is keeping you in California?" He said, sitting up on my hips and looking down at me.

I blinked as I thought through his question. Nothing, really. My parents had died years ago, leaving my brother and me on our own. Jackson was living in Europe, so it certainly wasn't family. Sure, I had friends, but I could still visit.

"That's right. Nothing." Rylie said. I noticed he was careful not to touch me, other than where his hips straddled mine. "Do you want to take the position?"

I looked at him, trying to understand what he was really asking. "Taking me completely out of the equation. If we were not a thing, would you take the job?"

"Yes. It's job advancement, and I could easily support myself and have a nice comfortable life on that kind of money."

"Then take it and move in with me. Stay with me, Lucille Adaline."

"What?" I whispered.

Rylie got up and went to his bag, and as I sat up on the bed, he crouched down before me. He pulled me to him, and kissed me in a soft lingering kiss that made my toes curl. His voice caught, but he said, "You handled that bombshell I threw on you with a grace that I didn't expect. I had planned to have things happen in a completely different order this weekend. I was going to pull out all the stops. Wine and dine you all weekend. I wanted to do this the second I saw you at the airport, but..."

"Rylie..." My heart was thumping so hard I wasn't sure he couldn't hear it.

He opened a small box with a simple oval diamond and two smaller stones on the sides of it. "You are just Luci. I am just Rylie. Stay. Stay with *me*. Will you marry me?"

My eyes went wide as they filled with tears. I met his gaze and saw the longing and fear there.

"Me?" He nodded, and I asked, "You are serious? Before everything that happened last night, you had been planning to ask me to marry you?"

"I was. Like I said, I wanted this weekend to go completely different from the way it has, but in the end, I want you. So, I ask again, Lucille Adaline Baker, will you do me the honor of being my wife?"

"Yes." The words were out immediately. There was nothing to think about when it came to Rylie, because he was right. I was just Luci, and he was just Rylie.

With a long-relieved breath, he pulled the ring out and put it on my shaking hand. My head was in his hands, and he was kissing me again. "Thank God."

"You were worried I would say no?"

"I kept a huge secret from you for a year. So, yes, I thought you would walk out and I would never see you again. Instead, you sat on my lap and kissed me stupid." He kissed me again, and I wrapped my legs around his hips, pulling him closer.

My alarm went off then, and I sighed. "I want to stay in bed with you. All day. Show you all the ways you are so very wrong. I want nothing more than to wake up in your arms every single day until my last breath, Rylie James."

His phone pinged repeatedly with text messages then, and his eyebrows knitted when he checked them. A few texts flew back and forth, and he let out a heavy sigh.

"Need to take care of some things?" I asked.

"Yeah. You'll be what, three-four hours? Done by lunch?"

I nodded. "That's the plan. My meeting with Ray Henderson is at ten. Hopefully, he will sign the contract. Sam says he will if I agree to the position. Apparently, I'm part of the negotiations."

"Ray Henderson? As in Henderson and Sons?"

"Yes?" He studied me for a long moment. "What is it Rylie?"

His mouth opened and closed a couple times before I raised my eyebrows at him and raised my left hand up, twinkling the ring on my finger. "Absolutely no secrets, Rylie James Allen."

"That is the Henderson project you would personally oversee?"

"It is." I drawled. "What is your connection to Henderson and Sons?"

"They are a pretty large client. More importantly, Ray Henderson's son is Malk."

"Malk is Malcom Henderson. How had I not put that together?" I smacked my forehead. They had been friends since he moved out here. Rylie and Malk had gotten closer after Harper's death. It had really torn Malk up, too.

"You've seen pictures of him, Luce." He chuckled. "Though I never use his full name. Let alone his last name. It never would have come up. Since I, ya know, hid the whole business side of my life from you for so long."

I shook my head, but then I got to thinking, and I pressed my lips together.

"I know that look. You aren't happy." He stood before me and lifted my chin so I was looking at him. "What is it, sweetheart?"

"Our relationship is public now. It won't be long before it breaks that we are engaged, because I'm not going to hide that. Yes, I want to protect our privacy, but let the world know that Rylie Allen is taken. Solidly taken."

"Damn fucking right, he is." He said, bending down and kissing me softly. "So fucking taken."

I smiled, blushed slightly before sighing, "But I'm not going to have our relationship and my connection to you dictate things at work. I have worked very hard in this very male-dominated field to get where I am."

"I won't say anything to Malk before your contract is signed."

"If he texts you to ask who the woman was on your arm last night?" I said teasingly, as I ran a finger down his bare chest to his bellybutton.

"He already has, and I've ignored him." When I gave him a look, he pushed a few buttons on his phone and showed me a text chain.

Malk Henderson:

Who was that beautiful woman at dinner man?

Don't you ignore me, fucker. Who was she?

I can't believe you've kept a woman like that a secret.

How did you do it?

Rylie Allen. I can see you've read these. Answer me.

I chuckled. "If he is talking to you like that…"

"Yeah. The best friend is a bit pissed." I raised an eyebrow at him and he just shrugged. "He's a good man. His father is too."

"Seriously though, if I take this job, I don't want connections to be a benefit. I know the second I become Lucille Adaline Allen, it won't matter, but…"

His gaze heated as he said, "Fuck, I like the sound of that."

"Rylie." I said, drawing out his name.

"I will not tell him the connection." His phone went off again, and he chuckled. "Though I have a feeling, he will know the second he walks into that meeting with you and Sam this morning."

"Seriously? He's going to be there?" I groaned. "Not exactly how I expected to meet Malk in person."

"I wish you could have met him last time you were here, but he was running a project in North Carolina for a while. I rarely saw him, myself."

I looked over at the clock, then down at the ring on my left hand. I blinked, and took a few breaths, before saying, "I have to be there in an hour to discuss my new position."

My eyes flicked to him, and his eyes softened. "Seriously, take it or don't. Either way, come and move into my place."

"I don't..."

"Luce. You just agreed to be my wife. Why not just move in now? It's one less move you have to make in the next year or so."

"You sure?" I asked, but memories from years ago flew through my head. I shrank down into myself again, and Rylie was there.

"I could kill him for this." He growled. "Sweetheart. You are Queen of my domain. What *you* say goes. I will not control you. I will not belittle you. You know that. I think you also know I have proven to you I will do nothing but cherish every hair on your body and destroy anyone who would even think to harm you."

His arms wrapped around me, and I found myself melting into him. I fought the shameful tears. "I'm sorry, Rylie. Every memory of what happened in that apartment just flew through my head in the matter of a second."

"Sweetheart. It's going to take a long time to undo that programming. I will be there every step of the way."

Rylie's thumbs moved back and forth to settle me down, and I found myself resting my head on his shoulder.

"Now, let's get in the shower. I want to drop you off, and then get this crap sorted at the office. I'll meet you back here when you're done, okay?"

I nodded, and let him carry me to the shower.

Chapter Eleven

"Good luck, sweetheart." Rylie said, as we made our way to the meeting room at the Kolvinal's Office building. There were a few double takes when I swiped my badge and Rylie opened the door for me, and I couldn't help the smile on my face. "I'll meet you back at the hotel, and then I'll prove to you, once again, just how much I worship the ground you walk on."

We made our way down the warm brick hall as my heels clicked on the white hardwood under our feet. Clocks hung on the wall, indicating the time in New York, Chicago, Denver, and Santa Clara. Each of our office locations. "No more surprises to spring on me?"

"Nope."

"You sure, Rye? Because I've been in Chicago for eighteen hours, and I've gotten a promotion, found out my boyfriend is the sole partner and CEO of Webster Enterprises, and... I'm forgetting something." I dramatically looked down at my hand and wiggled my fingers to make my new accessory sparkle in the recessed lighting above our heads. "Oh right, I got engaged to my boyfriend."

He bumped my hip as we walked, and I looked up and smiled at him. His eyes sparkled as he took that hand and threaded his fingers through mine. When we reached the meeting room, he leaned down and kissed my forehead. His lips lingered, and I was reveling in the feel of them, when I heard my name shouted in excitement.

I sighed and looked up at Rylie, who had an amused grin on his face. "You might as well come meet him now. He'll just hound me until the dawn of time, until you do."

Rylie huffed a laugh and put his hand on the small of my back as he guided me over to the meeting doors where Sam was waiting. "This will only be the first of a number of introductions over the next few months, Luce. It's fine. You are about to get a crash course in Rylie Allen."

"I think I know you pretty well. It's the world that doesn't know Rylie Allen." When we got to where Sam was standing, slack jawed, I said cheerfully, "Good morning, Sam."

Sam looked at me, looked at Rylie, opened his mouth, and when I smiled at Rylie, I said, "Rylie, this is Sam Bradford, my boss. Sam. This is Rylie Allen, my fiancé."

The words fell off my tongue like melted butter, and I couldn't help the amazing, warm feeling that flooded me.

"I really like the sound of that." Rylie said under his breath as he kissed the top of my head, and stretched his hand out to Sam. "Nice to meet you. I've heard a lot about you."

Sam looked to me and then to Rylie again, and in slow motion took Rylie's hand. When he recovered, he shook his head quickly, and said, "I'm sorry, I'm at a disadvantage here. I didn't even know Luci was involved with anyone, let alone the CEO of Webster Enterprises."

"We've known each other for a very long time." Rylie said smoothly. "We've also been pretty quiet about our relationship for a number of reasons."

Nodding, Sam looked at me and said, "This is why you were so protective during our conversation last night."

I stared at him pointedly and raised an eyebrow. "It is. Until recently, my private life was my own. I realize that now that it is public knowledge that Rylie and I are together, our lives won't be private, but I want to keep as much of it as possible that way." I took a steadying breath before saying, "Let me make one thing crystal clear. My relationship with Rylie Allen has nothing to do with my work. There will be no special favors, no media ploys, nothing."

"Of course." Sam said, his eyes flicking to Rylie.

"I know you two have much to talk about. I'll let you get to it." Then Rylie turned, kissed me quick and ran his thumb over the ring now on my finger and whispered as he leaned forward to kiss the top of my head, "No fair being the first one to introduce us as engaged." He pulled back and there was a wide smile on his face. I just stuck my tongue out at him, and he shook his head.

"Have a good day, Sam." Then he was walking off. The way he walked out, head high, shoulders back, and his hands in his pockets... It was like he didn't have a care in the world. I watched him as he went through the double doors and pulled his phone out.

"Rylie Allen." He said with a light whistle. "Luci, you never cease to amaze me."

"So, the Henderson project." I said, blatantly ignoring the comment, as I strode past him, and toward the maps and drawings on the table. I took off my jacket and hung it over the chair. Rylie had picked out my outfit, and dressed me again this morning, and I had to admit I felt business beautiful in it. He had chosen a simple knee-length skirt paired with a lightweight v-neck sweater and nude pumps.

"First, I need your answer. I have HR on the line." He pushed a couple buttons on a remote, and the Director of HR and two others showed up on the video conference window on the TV on the right side of the room.

I stood up and crossed my arms. "David. Good to see you again."

"Ms. Baker." David's eyes shifted as if he was looking for someone else in the room.

"Are you looking for someone in particular?" I raised an eyebrow at the Director of HR.

"There have been some," He cleared his throat, and I interrupted him.

"Photos of me with a certain CEO of Webster Enterprises?" I raised my eyebrows, waiting for his answer.

"Well, yes." There was something oddly satisfying about seeing the Director of HR shift uncomfortably in his seat.

I took a deep breath and maintained a professional demeaner, even though I wanted nothing more than to roll my eyes. "Rylie Allen and I have been friends for a very long time. I fail to see how this has anything to do with the reason we're here."

"The photos released on social media overnight indicate more than friends." There was a tentative nature to his voice that told me he was trying to ask more without directly asking the question. I kept my face neutral.

This was the first of a long list of lines I was going to draw in the sand. Hold your boundaries.

I took a long breath and said firmly, but professionally, "Mr. Allen isn't here, nor should he be part of this conversation. We are here to discuss my business life, not my personal life. That being said, don't believe everything you read and see in the press gossip section. If I did something that violates company policy, or if my work performance and ability to complete the Henderson project or other projects in a timely manner has diminished in any way because my personal life, then, and only then, do I need to make you aware of my personal life."

There was a quick nod, and David cleared his throat before he looked to Sam, who just gave him a quick nod. "Very well, I assume Sam provided you with the information about the offer last night?"

"He did." I wanted to keep this quick and short if I could. They didn't know the development that my personal life had taken, and I tried to hide my hand in hopes they wouldn't notice the accessory on my left hand.

"An additional 40K a year, your full-time residency in Chicago,—"

"As I said, Sam went through the details with me last night. I've already decided to accept, should the following conditions also be met." I met David's eye through the monitor and said, "My personal life will *not* be used for company in any way, be it publicity, advertisement, or boasting ability of connections. I will not use my personal connections with Webster Enterprises to help Kolvinal in any professional way, shape, or form. You will continue as you had been before the news of my personal connection with Mr. Rylie Allen broke last night. If, at any time, I feel my connections are being used, or that special treatment in any way is being used or given, I will walk, immediately."

Another window popped up, and when I saw who it was, I was only mildly surprised to see him show up. "Mr. Kolvinal." I said in greeting.

"And what does Mr. Allen think—"

I let out a frustrated breath out of my nose. "This is the last time I'm going to comment on this before filing a harassment claim with HR. Mr. Allen has no say in what I do with my work. Mr. Allen doesn't work for Kolvinal, I do."

"What if our office has a business relationship with Webster Enterprises in the future?" Chantel, Sam's boss, said.

"Then you will assign him a representative, other than Luci Baker, and treat him with the same respect and attention we give all our clients." Sam's voice was restrained, and I could tell he was trying to hold back his own frustration.

When no one said anything else, I eyed each of them in the camera, and said, "I have given you my terms and I have agreed to become the punching bag for the Henderson project, but these are my conditions."

"Punching bag?" Chantel's head tipped to the side in question.

There was no holding back my eye roll this time. "We all know that should anything go wrong, there will be negative press, or there is a dumpster fire somewhere along the lines of this project, it will be thrown at my feet. You can't tell me I won't be the one who takes the heat." I took a deep breath to settle myself, and said, "I understand the responsibility, clout, and income this project will bring to the company. I also know that I'm one of the best at what I do, and therefore the best person for the job. Are we in agreement?"

"We agree to your terms, Ms. Baker." Mr. Kolvinal said.

I let the corner of my mouth lift. "Now, is there anything else I can do for you this morning?"

"Will you be extending your stay to look for new accommodations?" Mr. Kolvinal said.

"I already have a few vacation days at the end of this trip." I took a deep breath. "After that, I'm scheduled for Houston."

He at least was polite about it, and just nodded before saying, "Hold onto your vacation days. Consider this weekend paid overtime for the purpose of securing your new living accommodations. We will reschedule the Houston meeting for later in the month. That should allow you time to pack and move, assuming Henderson signs the contract today."

"He will." I said firmly, shooting a pointed look at Sam.

Chapter Twelve

Twenty minutes later, Sam and I had gone over every aspect of the preliminary sketches and drawings that we had done to prove that we were the right company for this contract with Henderson and Sons. When there was a knock on the door, I straightened and waited for Sam to open it.

Ray Henderson walked in, greeted Sam, and then his son, Malk, and Jason, the Henderson's Project Manager walked in. I almost didn't recognize Malk in a suit and tie. In all the pictures he had been in with Rylie, he had always been in a t-shirt, jeans, and a ballcap. He was usually muddy from head to toe since he and Rylie often went four-wheeling. We had spoken on the phone a couple of times, but I didn't really know him.

Neither looked at me until Sam said, "Ray, Malcom, I'd like to introduce you to your personal representative, Luci Baker. I know Jason has been working with her, but I don't believe you two have formally met."

I looked at Jason, who smiled at the looks on Ray Henderson and Malk's faces. Jason had obviously put it together overnight and not warned them. "Nice to see you again, Jason."

"I'm going to fucking smack Rylie so fucking hard." Raising an eyebrow at him, I tried to hold back a laugh, which came out more like a huffed snort. "I'm sorry, Luci."

"Hi, Malk." I turned to his father and said, "Nice to meet you, Mr. Henderson."

He reached out his hand and said, "It's nice to meet you too, Ms. Baker." He looked at Malk and I noticed his eyes widen just the slightest amount.

Sam looked at me and smiled as he turned back to Mr. Henderson. "It is clear from the look on your faces that you have seen the abundance of social media that broke overnight."

"The media can be a bit dramatic." Mr. Henderson said, carefully.

"But Rylie could have at least given me a fucking heads up. I've been texting him all morning."

He reached into his pocket and pulled his phone out as I said with a small smile, "I'm aware."

He froze as my words sank in.

I looked at the three of them, and when Sam stood at my side, he nodded. He was letting me run this show. If I was going to be their personal fall girl, then I was going to show them where the boundaries were. "As I've told Kolvinal, I have agreed to be your personal rep here in Chicago, not because of Rylie Allen, but because I am damn good at my job. That and you have personally requested me," I said, looking at Mr. Henderson.

"At Jason's insistence. He has done nothing but boast about your abilities to handle anything that we have thrown at you." He looked at Jason and asked, "And you didn't know of Mr. Allen's association with Ms. Baker?"

"Not until I saw the media this morning. Wasn't exactly sure how to mention it, since, as you said, the media can be dramatic." Jason said cautiously.

I maintained my power stance at the end of the table. "As I was saying, since you have personally requested that I handle your account, I have chosen to accept the offer." I indicated the drawings on the table and said, "Now, would you like to go over the preliminary drawings? Since you received the contract two weeks ago from our Legal Department, I'm assuming you have had your lawyers look through it."

"We have, and we are agreeable to the terms. I'm going to assume that you want to ensure that any association with Webster Enterprises is kept completely separate from those of Kolvinal's?"

"That would be correct. I will not call in special favors for any security tech or any other supplies that would be purchased from Webster Enterprises."

He smiled and said, "Well, since I'm already invested in Webster Enterprises, it would make sense that I continue to support their business ventures. That was already something lined up, long before we walked into this meeting today."

I looked at Malk and sighed. "I realize that since you and Rylie are friends, we are going to see a lot of each other outside of professional situations. This goes without saying, but with some of the conversations

I've already had to have today, I'm going to mention how much I would appreciate your confidentiality and attempt at keeping our private lives private." My attention shifted to Sam and then to Mr. Henderson. "This is, assuming Mr. Henderson signs the contract."

"I've already signed it and have it ready for you. I assumed Sam could secure your employment for the projects." Ray took it from his pocket and plopped it on the conference table. Mr. Henderson turned and smiled at me. "The campuses each have their own specialty right? Medical supplies, paper production, rock and concrete, and electrical?

I nodded as Sam went to the contract and initialed the last few places, sealing my fate. "It's an undertaking, but it will be a great boost for the economy. You will be bringing in a lot of trade skill based jobs."

"We will work with the sales department to diversify the distribution. It was going to be mainly used for Webster Enterprises, but I can see the optics may not be great if we are ever audited."

"There are some changes to at least one of the campuses that Malcom would like to make." Jason indicated the plans on the table with a nod of his head and offered me a friendly smile. I nodded back to him, and let out a small breath in relief.

Malk came to stand next to me, and with a small smile said, "Rylie and I were talking about funding an onsite education program. Work with the local high schools as a paid ROP program or something. We haven't worked out all the kinks on it yet."

I walked over to the table and thumbed through the plans and asked, "Which ones?"

"Pilsen and Goose Island. Which will be medical and paper, respectively."

When I found the campus drawings I was looking for, I laid them out flat and Jason came over and pointed to a few suggested spots. Malk looked down and when he saw the ring on my finger, his eyes went wide.

I lifted my finger to my lips and let the corner of my lips raise when he gave me a questioning look. Malk shook his head and ran his hand over his face. His eyes met mine, and he smiled, and mouthed a "Congratulations."

I smiled softly, and whispered a "thank you" before Jason said, "Ideally, there should be a tech school on each campus, but these two locations are good places to start."

"They are the first two scheduled to break ground, right?"

"That's the plan." Jason ran his hand through his hair and scratched his chin. Jason and I talked for a few minutes, sorting out a few more details, when Malk stepped away, reaching for his phone. Then I heard him behind me saying, "You fucking dick twat."

I giggled as Jason huffed a laugh. "Poor, Rylie."

"Yeah. I wouldn't want to be him right now." I said as I looked over to where Sam and Mr. Henderson were going over some other projects. I snorted a laugh when I saw Mr. Henderson's eyes staring wide eyed at Malk.

Mr. Henderson chastised him, "Professionalism, Malcom." Unfortunately, Malk just rolled his eyes at his father. The man had guts, that's for sure.

He had lowered his voice, but he said, "Yeah imagine the surprise I had when I walked in and saw your girl is the one we've been working with for months... Asshole... There is even a... I mean congratulations and all, but a little warning." I tried very hard not to fist my hand and bring attention to it. Let Mr. Henderson and Jason come to their own conclusions."

"Luci, his royal asshole, wants to talk to you." He said, handing me the phone.

"Separation, Rye." I said evenly, and pointed to a spot on the plans that I thought might work, and gave Jason a raised eyebrow in question.

"Malcom, put your VP pants on and come look at the plans." Jason told Malk.

Rylie's chuckle came through the phone, and I took a deep breath. "I know, sweetheart. I'm sorry."

"Malk's gonna have to figure his shit out. Any of your other friends that I should be worried about having this kind of reaction? He's throwing a bit of a hissy fit over not knowing about me."

"Let him." He said, but then his voice dropped and he said, "Cuz as long as I have you, I don't care."

"I thought we settled that this morning." I said softly, thumbing the ring on my finger.

"We did, and I didn't get to worship you properly afterwards, either."

I hummed into the phone.

"I should have just pushed you against the shower wall and fucked you senseless."

I took a deep breath, letting it out slowly through my nose at the mental image that created. I could practically feel his fingers digging into my ass as he held me against the wall and pounded into me. My voice was thick as I shifted on my feet, and said, "I think I'm already senseless if I agreed to all this." I stepped further away and stood in front of the windows at the other end of the room.

"It's too late now. You will be Mrs. Allen. Maybe I'll just start calling you that in front of everyone. Get you used to it."

"I thought I was just Luci, and you were just Rylie." I whispered, trying to keep my voice down, and the image of Rylie owning me in the shower out of my head.

"Oh, we are in the privacy of our own home. When you are writhing under me, and screaming my name..."

"Oh, dear heavens." I whispered, and I felt myself quiver at the way he said that.

"Hurry up. I'll see you soon. I want to have my fiance's pussy for lunch."

"I'm sorry, what?" I mumbled and flipped my head around, scanning the room to make sure that no one else heard our conversation.

"You heard me." He hummed a moment and said, "One day, I'll lay you out over my desk here, have a full course meal, then fuck that beautiful ass as you moan my name for the whole building to hear."

I took a shuddering breath and said, "I'll hold you to that, but for now, I do have to find a way to get my wits back so I can finish this meeting. I'll see you soon."

His throaty chuckle came through as he said, a little too heated, "I love you."

"Love you too, Rye." I said, as the call disconnected. I fisted my hands and took a couple deep breaths. I knew my cheeks were more than a few too many shades of red at the moment.

I was just thinking I might have my wits about me, when Malk came over and I handed him his phone. "Please, Malk, professionalism in the future?"

"Of course, Luci. I'm sorry. You made it pretty clear that you wanted to keep your..." He looked down to the ring on my finger and said, "Association with my best friend quiet and separate."

"As much as possible. I realize that with Rylie being the CEO of Webster Enterprises, and that his best friend is Malcom Henderson..." I looked at him evenly. "Do you have any idea how stupid I feel for not putting that together?"

"Rylie and I can just be two dudes when we go four wheeling. We ignore all the weight of the businesses and just... have fun. It's nice to have a friend like that."

I smiled at him. "He's lucky to have you. After Harper..."

"It was hard on all of us when Harper died. Most of all, Rylie. I wasn't sure how he was able to make it through, but every time he'd go to California, he'd always come back so much more grounded. More of the man I think he wanted to be." He looked at me carefully and said,

"Now, seeing that rock on your hand. I think that was because of you. I'm happy for you two. If you need anything, let me know."

"Thanks. Now let's go over the sketches and see where we can put yours and Rylie's trade school." I jerked my head toward the table.

"Professionalism, Ms. Baker." He jokingly admonished.

Chapter Thirteen

When I got back to the room, Rylie wasn't there, but when I flopped down on the now made bed. I stretched and yawned a bit too loud, and half wanted to just nap before he got back. Just when I was thinking that would be the best option, my fingers hit paper on one of the pillows. I looked up to find a note.

I got up and looked at the Webster Enterprises stationary, with 'Sweetheart' written on the front of it in Rylie's handwriting. Ripping the envelope open, I read the quick note.

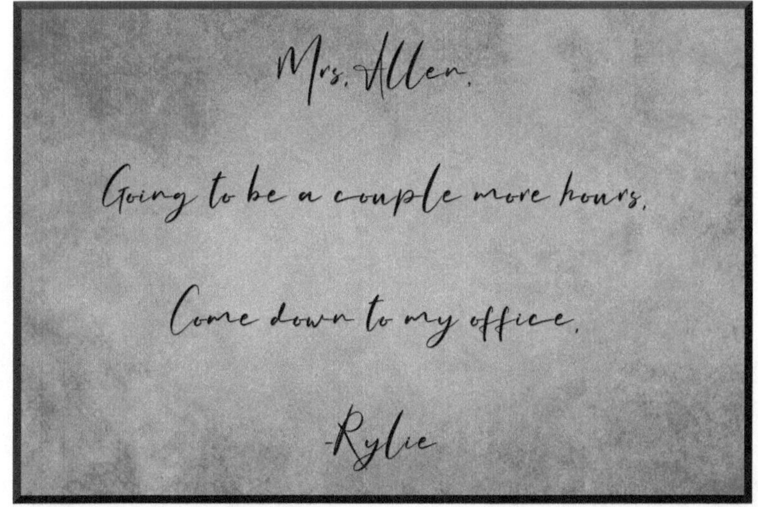

I sighed, grabbed my jacket and purse, and headed downstairs. I walked out, and headed toward the river knowing the Webster Enterprises office building was only a few blocks from the hotel.

I stopped dead in my tracks though when I got a whiff of coffee from the shop on the corner. Okay, coffee first, then Rylie. Priorities had to be met. He was still finishing up, anyway.

When I walked in, I headed straight for the counter, and placed my order. I stood off to the side, and noted the scrolling social media feed on the wall.

I blinked. Over half of them were of Rylie and I arriving at the restaurant last night. The others were various angles of me on his lap and kissing him, us walking out the front doors or of my freak out heading to the car.

"Who is Rylie Allen's woman?" One post said.

"CEO of Webster Enterprises, steps out with unknown woman for the first time." Another scrolled by.

Even BMT had their feed saying, "Tech giant was cozy with mysterious woman last night at *Embers Incongnito.*"

The news screen flashed, and the anchor said, "The news everyone is talking about this morning. Just who was that woman on the arm of Rylie Allen last night?"

I pulled my hood up over my head, and was half embarrassed and half mad at the reoccurring shot of me sitting on his lap, kissing him.

We had talked about it, joked about it even, but to see it scroll by as if it was the best story of the day... then realization hit me. For the business socialite world, it *was* the news of the day. The new CEO had never been seen with anyone. No flings. No one. We were big news. Rylie Allen, CEO of Webster Enterprises and the unnamed nobody.

I took a deep breath, and just tried to remember it would blow over soon. I looked down and saw the ring on my finger and smiled. The news would lose interest in my nobodiness by tomorrow. Deep breaths, in and out.

"Luci! Grande Espresso Macchiato." The barista called, and I stepped forward to collect my latte, and when she handed it to me, she froze. Her eyes flicked to the screen, then to me.

"Please don't." I whispered, and met her gaze. She nodded, and I quickly mouthed a thank you, took my drink, and rushed out.

I somehow made every crosswalk between the hotel and the river where Webster Enterprises Corporate building was. When I got to the corner with a single tree planted out front, I took a deep breath and looked up to an extraordinarily tall glass building. I silently cursed Rylie, but opened the glass doors and strode across the polished stone foyer up to the welcome desk. As I waited for the red headed receptionist to finish with the person in front of me, I took a sip of my coffee and jumped when she said, "Can I help you?"

"Yes. Can you tell me which floor Rylie's office is on?"

"Do you have an appointment?" She snapped her gum and I shuddered.

"Not one that would be on the books." I said nicely, and as professionally as I could.

"Mr. Allen doesn't see people without an appointment. Please call, make an appointment, and return with your confirmation code."

I sighed, and said, "Can you please call his desk and tell him that Luci is here. And that you are sending his girl up?"

"No ma'am. Please make an appointment and return with your confirmation code." She eyed me with a quick derogatory up and down, and then the people behind me before saying, "Mr. Allen doesn't have *girls.*"

She had said it like she had personally been affronted by him. Now I was getting frustrated, but tried to realize she was just doing her job. "You need a confirmation code for me to be shown up to Mr. Allen's office?"

"Yes ma'am."

"Okay, hold on. I'll get the ultimate pass." I pulled out my phone, hit the video call button, and turned around so that he could see me and the receptionist in the frame.

"Hey, sweetheart. You here yet?" He answered.

"I am. Rylie, can you please tell the receptionist to let me in and where exactly is your office? It's not like I've been here before."

He chuckled, and my eye met the receptionist behind me through the phone screen. She looked like she was about to pass out.

"Alexandrea, please let my fiance in. I'll have security meet her at the elevators." He gestured off screen, and then said, "Now hurry up. I need you."

I just smirked at him, and hung up.

"I'm sorry ma'am. Right this way, please." She said, and walked with me to the elevators, where a tall thin man stood.

"Ms. Baker, I'm Kevin. I'm here to escort you directly to Mr. Allen." He held his arm open to keep the doors from closing, and when a few people tried to come in as well, he shook his head.

When the doors closed, I asked, "Why couldn't they come with? This elevator is large enough for twenty people."

He huffed a chuckle and said, "Because I am taking you non-stop to the 35th floor, ma'am. Straight up."

I blinked, and then the cab was moving up. After a moment, I grabbed his arm, and squeezed tight.

"Don't like elevators, ma'am?"

"It's a California earthquake thing. I'm not a fan of tall buildings, either." I took a deep breath and just whispered, "I'm going to kick your fucking ass, Rylie."

Kevin chuckled, and let me hold on to him the entire way up. When it dinged, I released a long breath, released my hand, but noticed there was blood from my nails on his forearm.

"I'm sorry." I said, and he looked at me curiously. "About your arm. And about you having to come down to get me."

"It's no problem. If it makes you feel any better, I've had much worse. This way, please." He led me through a huge open office, where everyone's eyes seemed to trail me as I walked toward a set of double doors. Outside was a glass office where Kevin stopped and said, "I'm taking her straight in, Janette."

The woman looked up, met my eye, and nodded. Kevin opened the door, and ushered me through it, closing the door behind me. Rylie was facing the window, and talking on the phone.

"Yes, I know." He sighed and said, "Well, she's off limits... I don't care. Get Luci off the social media feeds. I don't want her face plastered everywhere. Not until she is ready."

My heart warmed because I knew why he was being so protective. I looked at the desk that was between the two of us, and smiled at the memory of what he had said on the phone earlier. Finding some bravery, I slipped my shoes off, ensured the door was indeed locked, and quietly undressed.

I tiptoed across the hardwood floor to stand behind him, wrapped my arms around his waist, and leaned against him. His hand caressed my arm, but he looked down when he noticed it was bare. Since he helped dress me this morning, he knew exactly what I had been wearing. Flipping around, he took half a step back and blinked.

"I need to go. Something came..." He looked me up and down, and a devilish smirk crossed his face. "Up. I need to take care of this. Do your job, please. Just make her face disappear. Protect Luci's identity. That is your number one responsibility for now."

He pushed the button on his headset and threw it off toward the other end of the room. He hit a button on his desk, and another layer of doors came down.

"Fuck. I should have you come by the office more often." He said, pulling me to him and kissing along my jaw.

Chapter Fourteen

Keeping my eyes on his as I undid his tie and let it fall to the floor, I tilted my head back and to the side when he started kissing my neck, and pulling my hips to his. I felt him pressing against his slacks, and when I palmed him, he jumped back.

"Now, now. Just because you strolled in here and caught me off guard doesn't mean you have control, sweetheart."

He gripped my hips and lifted me onto the edge of his desk. He pushed the files and keyboard off with a single swipe of his arm, everything landing on the floor with a crash, and pushed me back to lay down. He ran a finger through the center of me and I jumped when he flicked my clit before taking that finger and sticking it into his mouth.

"Thank you for bringing lunch." He cooed.

"Lunch?"

"I did say I wanted your pussy for lunch. Did I not?"

"You did." I breathed, my heart suddenly racing.

He licked his lips as he stripped off his shirt. I couldn't help admiring the way his muscles moved as he pulled it off and threw it to the side. His hands grabbed both of my thighs, and when he bent down, he threw my legs over his shoulders.

I was wide open for him, and he hummed a satisfied sound before he ran his tongue languidly in circles around my clit. I closed my eyes, and reveled in the feel of him exploring every inch of exposed flesh between my legs. It wasn't long before he was diving in and tongue fucking me, while fingering my clit.

"Fuck me, Rylie." I reached down and ran my hands through his hair, widening my legs to allow him more access. I felt his laughter and when I looked down at him, he was watching me intently.

I was getting so close to release, and he knew it. He clamped down on my clit, and finger fucked me with abandon. When a finger pressed against my rosebud, I screamed in pleasure as that orgasm blew through me.

Rylie's motions slowed as I subsided, and when he leaned down to kiss me, the scruff of his beard shone with my release. The taste of me on his lips, made my stomach tighten again.

"Now, I'm sure you are famished." He said, pulling me up and off of the desk. I looked at him hopefully and flicked my eyes to where his cock was straining to be released from its restraints. A raised eyebrow was his only instruction. I fell to my knees and freed him, taking the head of him into my mouth, before I had even slipped his pants off his hips.

I ran my tongue around the head and rolled my tongue on that spot under the rim of him. When I curled through the slit, his moan flowed over me. His hands rested on my head, and I hummed as I swallowed him. I only adjusted slightly to allow him down my throat, and hummed again.

"For all that is holy, Luce." His knees buckled slightly, causing him to fall from my lips. I whimpered, and when I grasped ahold of him again, he said, "I love the way your face shines with my cock in your mouth."

"Then fuck it." I whispered, looking up to him through my eyelashes. I ran the head of him along my lips as I awaited his answer.

"Who am I to deny you?" It was his only warning as he thrust his cock down my throat, pulled out, thrusted again, and held himself there. My tongue lashed out at his balls and I hummed. He twitched within me before he pulled out and thrust down repeatedly in long steady strokes. Rylie picked up the pace, and just when I thought I would be able to enjoy the feel of his cum sliding down my throat, he pulled out, pulled me up, kissed me quickly, smacked my ass and said, "Turn around."

I didn't argue as he said, "Brace yourself on the desk." Then he slammed into me. The initial shock of being so incredibly full of Rylie came out in a ravaged moan. There was no adjusting period, just Rylie slamming into me over and over again. My hand slipped, and I readjusted.

"I said to brace yourself." He said, leaning down and kissing my shoulder while grinding into me.

"Rylie, just fuck me."

"Am I not doing enough?" He pulled out, and then punched back into me, at the same time as he smacked my ass hard.

My answering moan was quickly masked by the sound of another smack. "Or maybe my girl just wants her ass fucked?"

He pulled out of me, and then his tongue was circling my rosebud, and I couldn't help the pleading moan that came from me. "Is that what you want, sweetheart? Me to fuck your ass?"

Smack!

"Sweetheart?" He didn't wait for my answer, before another smack came down and I moaned as he ran a finger up the middle of me, and finger fucked me.

Smack!

"Rylie..."

Smack!

Then the sound of a desk drawer opening and closing. Smack!

Cold liquid trailed over my asshole, and I quivered in anticipation. His fingers worked the lube over, around, and within me, and when his fingers twitched deep within me, I had to bite my tongue.

"Oh, yes, my girl likes her ass played with, doesn't she?"

"Rylie, please. I need to cum." Every nerve in my body was on fire. I wasn't sure how much more I could take.

A moment later, I felt him press the head of his cock into my ass, and when I pressed back against him, there was an amused chuckle. Once he was buried within me, I rolled my hips against him, and heard him moan himself.

I pulled away from him and then fell back against him, feeling his balls slap against my clit. The feeling of it had me concentrating on not falling over that edge.

The groan that came from Rylie though was guttural and animalistic. He lifted my hips to his, "Better hold on sweetheart."

He pounded into me relentlessly. I was pushing back against him at every hard thrust. "Fuck yes, Luci. Your ass feels so good. Rub your clit, sweetheart. I want to hear you cum for me."

I reached down and pinched my clit between my fingers, and when he pounded into me the next time, I was begging. "Rylie. Yes. Please."

I reached further down and stuck two fingers into me as he fucked my ass, and just as I fell over the edge, he reamed into me, and my braced hand gave out hitting the monitors, pushing them to the ground.

Only Rylie didn't stop. He continued to fuck me like a starved man. I once again, felt that tightening in my stomach, and continued to finger fuck myself. Rylie's cock twitched as he said, "That's my girl." And unloaded himself deep within me. The feel of his release had me reeling all over again. This time though when my orgasm subsided, my legs gave out from underneath me.

Rylie caught me and braced me against the desk. Bending over and kissing my shoulder, he slid from me and said, "Good girl. I'll be right back."

He disappeared into a little room off to the right I hadn't even noticed when I came in. He came out with a small washcloth and stopped short of his desk, looking me over. I curled my arms under my head and rested there a moment and asked, "Like what you see?"

"Very much. When I said I wanted to have you for lunch, I had pictured you sprawled out on my desk, but that image is nothing to the real thing." His eyes lingered a moment longer, then he took to cleaning me up. It was soft and gentle, in a way only Rylie had ever been.

CHAPTER FIFTEEN

Rylie held my sweater out, looking me over with an appreciative smile on his face. "I hate to get you dressed. I do appreciate you nude."

"As I do you." I slipped my arms into the sweater, and as he helped me slip it over my head, Rylie fondled my breasts before his hands trailed down to my waist, pulling me close. Lifting his hand, he cradled my cheek and brought me in for a sweet kiss.

His phone rang, and he declined the call. It rang again, and he declined it again. This time his cellphone rang, and I sighed, "Guess you should probably get that."

"I don't want to. I have more pressing matters." He said, pulling me close against him.

"You just fucked your fiance." I said, smiling, as I wrapped my arms around his shoulders.

"I really do love the sound of that." He kissed me softly, as his phone continued to ring. "Mrs. Luci Allen. Oh, how I will enjoy using that name."

"Don't you think you should get your phone? I can wait. I think I've distracted you enough. You need to finish up so we can leave."

"Oh, no." He said, his face becoming very serious. "I will never make love to you, fuck you, rail you, whatever term you want to use for when we have sex, and then go straight to a business call. You will come before all of this. Even if the company goes under, there are still accounts that were personally protected under Harpers Trust for my long-term life. So, you will *always* be first."

I blushed and didn't know what to say to that kind of declaration. I didn't feel I deserved it, but that was a discussion for another time. When the call went to voicemail for the third time, and started ringing again, I reached over and answered it, "Mr. Allen's phone. How can I help you?"

"Who is this?"

"Who is this?" I repeated back to them.

"I don't know who you are, but please hand the owner his phone." The male voice said on the other end of the line.

"I'm sorry, he is entirely wrapped up right now. Can I take a message?" I used every ounce of professionalism I could bring forth as Rylie slowly kissed down my neck and squeezed my ass. I smacked him lightly on the shoulder and he just bit down on mine, which had me smacking my hand over my mouth to keep a moan from escaping.

"Tell him that we have a problem." The male said, then barked orders about contacting BMT to stop the story. I froze.

"What is the problem?" My voice was hard and cold.

"I'm sorry ma'am. Considering I do not know who you are," I pulled the phone from my ear and pressed the speakerphone button and his voice came over so Rylie could hear too, "I will not divulge any additional information."

"I will repeat myself. What is the problem?" I pulled back from Rylie to give him a look to say something.

"What is it, Morgan?" Rylie said, a trace of worry in his voice.

"Sir, I received notice that Justin Devereux has sold a story to BMT. Word is there are some intimate details about Ms. Baker."

I froze. Every part of me froze. Rylie reached for the phone, took it off speaker phone and said, "What is he threatening to say?... Has the paperwork been served yet?"

I fell to the floor and curled up into a ball. My legs trembled, and I pulled back into myself as my hand started to shake.

"Rylie." My voice was too quiet. Too weak. Just like me. No. Not weak. Conditioned. I took long, slow deep breaths to release the band that was constricting against my chest.

I knew this was going to happen. We knew this was going to happen. How did he know already? We should have had more time to plan, to work out a way out of this. To find a way to get ahead of it.

I took slow, deep breaths. In and out. In and out.

"Make sure that every news outlet knows the order was signed and that we will pursue damages should that order be broken."

"Rylie!" I said, finding a way to move and take his hand. I looked at him with pleaful eyes and he instantly sat down on the floor, and encircled me. "It's okay sweetheart. I knew this was a possibility."

A small soft kiss on the top of my head. Then he was talking into the phone and growling, "Let him try. Handle it, Morgan. Make sure that they follow the order."

He hung up the phone and wrapped me up tighter against him. "It's okay, Luce."

"I figured he would show up eventually, but I thought we would have more time. We would at least be able to make a formal engagement announcement." I said it so quickly, and I felt my muscles shiver and shake under his hold.

"Luci, I need you to breathe." He turned me to face him and put my face in his hands. "I anticipated Justin trying to throw some bad press. Last week, I filed for a gag order for him and all media outlets. The Judge signed it two days ago."

I blinked, and took a deep breath. He looked me solidly in the eye again and repeated himself. "I have a gag order for him and all media outlets."

I blinked rapidly at him and said, "What?"

"Do I have to repeat myself, again?"

"No. I heard you. I guess I'm just not fully comprehending. No, that's not it either. I... I..."

"Words, sweetheart. I need you to use them. Properly." He huffed a laugh and brushed his thumbs along my cheeks, wiping away the tears that had fallen.

"You did that?" I asked, my voice small and tentative, but then a small smile fell on my lips as I said, "You were so sure that I was going to agree to marry you that you had a gag order in place against my ex and the media for when word got out?"

"No. I told you earlier. I thought you would walk out of my life forever for keeping this all from you." He kissed my brow now that I was breathing more evenly. "However, I knew we would be seen in public together before I asked you. I was planning on taking you to the rooftop and asking you there tomorrow night."

"Oh."

His eyebrow popped up, "Oh? That is all you have to say?"

"Rylie. I know nothing about the high-profile world you live in. Getting a gag order against Justin would have never crossed my mind. I had just assumed that we would deal with the fallout. I'm not worried about what he would say. I mean, I am not going to hide who I am."

"It's the degradation and abuse he put you through. The fact that your body still reacts to his conditioning is why I put the gag order in place. I want to protect you from this." He said studying me closely. I nodded once, as he said, "I know there is not a single thing he would say that would be true or be a problem. It's the lies and the mental wear that is going to wear on you."

"So, what happens now?" I asked, taking another deep breath to calm the nerves. The band had lifted from my chest, and I felt a little hollow.

"Morgan will ensure all the media outlets have a copy of the Judge's order. It will be accompanied with a letter from my lawyer that says that if any news breaks and the information is traced back to Justin, then they will be sued and held in contempt of the order."

"I'm sure that there will be someone who will listen to Justin." I said looking down and playing with my fingers.

Rylie nodded. "I wish it would stop it all, but it will give them pause to see if it's worth the risk."

"Thank you." I said and pulled up onto my knees and kissed him. His hand slid down my sides and wrapped around my waist as he kissed me back.

"There is no reason to thank me, Luci." He said softly. "You are mine. I will protect you with everything I have, because you are my everything."

His phone rang, and he just reached over and picked it up, "Allen." A long-relieved breath came from him. "Thank you, Morgan... Let me know."

When he hung up, he pulled me to my feet, and said, "BMT has agreed to the gag order, and will not be running the story. They have also canceled his payment."

I chuckled, "Why does the fact they are canceling his check make me feel better?"

"Because part of you is a vindictive woman?" He gave me a look as to dare me to contradict him.

"Yeah. Okay. Fine. Maybe a little." I said smiling at him and wrapping my arms around his waist again and resting my head on his chest. I listened to his heartbeat a moment before whispering, "Thank you."

"Anything for you sweetheart." He kissed the top of my head again, and said, "Are you okay for going to lunch? Or would you rather I have something brought in."

I studied him carefully, and he sighed, "I don't want to push you into the limelight if you aren't ready. I can get us out of the building without being seen, but once we get to a restaurant, there will be a media presence everywhere."

"Do you still need to finish things up here?"

"Got it done just as you called me from downstairs." He shook his head. "I forgot about the security protocols Janette has put into place to help prevent unwanted visitors. I should have given you a code. I'll have to have a talk with the reception department."

"The girl, Alexandrea?" He nodded and waited for me to continue, "Was really just doing her job, even if she was a little snooty, but I suspect there have been a number of women trying to get some alone time with you."

He lifted a shoulder like it didn't matter. "Calling me though, video chatting with me. That was clever." He kissed me. "Speaking of clever, I got a call from Malk. He was highly impressed with you earlier. He said he looks forward to working with you and apologized profusely for being such an embarrassment to Henderson and Sons. He didn't handle himself well."

I shrugged. "He was... a bit ... surprised to see the girl his best friend had been photographed with the night before, suddenly standing before him in a completely unrelated situation." I laughed at the memory of it. "You should have seen it."

"Maybe next time."

"Please don't let there be a next time. I'd like to meet Dustin, and anyone else you consider a close friend, but let's arrange an official meet and greet. Maybe have them all over for dinner."

"Well, you had met Malk before."

"No. I had spoken to him on the phone before with you, not actually met him in person. I had seen a few pictures of you two together, but neither of you were exactly mud free." I smacked his chest, but a disappointing thought crossed my mind. "How had he never seen a picture of me?"

"He has. Lots of them. I showed him pictures of us with our friends back home."

"Had you not told him you were even involved?"

He smiled sadly, "Not directly. It's not that I was hiding you, I just didn't want you to become a media thing. I guess I didn't come out and say it with Malk, but I thought I had at least led on that you were special."

"Why not?"

"I am surprised he didn't put it together really. I'd shown him plenty of pictures of us with our arms around each other. Pictures of just the two of us. I really don't know how he hadn't figured it out." He helped me to stand and said, "I'm sorry I didn't come straight out and tell Malk about us."

I gave him a look that meant that he should have. "I don't like that I was a secret, Rye, because you never have been. All our friends knew we were together. Sure, I kept my private life quiet, but all our friends knew about us."

"Exactly. All of our friends knew. I should have trusted Malk to tell him everything about you, I just... I'm sorry sweetheart. I should have done better."

I studied him for a long moment and said, "I'll forgive you only because the look on his face this morning was so hilarious."

"I'm serious." He lifted my hand and fingered my engagement ring. "I would do it differently. This whole weekend was supposed to be way more spectacular for you."

"You mentioned that." I squeezed his hand and my stomach growled.

Rylie chuckled, and said, "Let's go back to the hotel and have some food delivered. I think you've had enough excitement for one day."

Chapter Sixteen

When we pulled up to the hotel, it was surrounded by media. Security verified our room key before letting us into the parking garage, and more security met us after we parked.

"Mr. Allen. I'm sorry for the swarm of media." The hotel manager said when Rylie opened the door for me to get out.

Rylie nodded, looked at me and said, "Do you want to stay here, or just pack up and head back to the condo?"

"They figured out who I am at this point. Does it matter if we try to hide?" I reached up and kissed him while we waited for the elevator. "You staying with me over the last year has seemed to work out for you. I'm sorry it doesn't anymore."

He just smiled, pushed my hair behind my ear, ran his finger over where his ring sat on my finger, and said, "I should have handled all this better with you. I should have told you before thrusting you in front of the cameras. I should have made sure you were okay with all this beforehand."

The door opened, and we stepped in. He pulled me close before he hit the button and rested his cheek on the top of my head. I held him tighter and said, "What's done is done. We can't take it back. I said yes to marrying you, Rylie. I have to accept this. It is a way of your life."

"But—"

"Stop." I said pulling back and looking up at him. "You can if, who, what, when, where, why, how, coulda, woulda, shoulda yourself to death. It won't change a damn thing."

"I just..." He trailed off when he saw the look on my face. "Okay. I'm sorry regardless."

"We have established that." The elevator dinged, and I strode out leaving him to follow. Yes, it would have been nice, but I didn't lie to him when I said it wouldn't have mattered. It doesn't matter. Sure, it complicates things. We won't have a quiet life, and I guess I will have to learn to watch my mouth, but I loved Rylie. I wasn't going to let this get in our way.

My stomach growled again as I was opening the door, and Rylie chuckled. "You sure you don't want to get some room service here while we pack?"

"I'd like to go and get settled at your place—"

"Our place." Rylie corrected.

"How is it that I've never been to your..." He raised his eyebrow at me, and I sighed, "Our place. That is going to take some getting used to saying."

"It was easier for me to keep that side of myself hidden from you. Easier to keep the media off *us*."

"That's why you've always been so insistent upon just staying at the hotel with me the last six months?" He nodded. I threw my suitcase open, and started packing my things. I had vaguely wondered about it, but figured he was just treating it as a mini vacation. A place away from home.

When all of our things were packed up, I took another look around the room, and there was a part of me that sighed sadly. "What's wrong?"

"Just thinking how this is the last of what was."

He came to stand behind me, wrapped his arms around my waist, and rested his chin on the top of my head. "We can still have these getaways. They will be a little harder to arrange, but it can be done. Are you ready to start a new chapter?"

"Yes. No." I said, leaning back against him and breathing him in. "Yes. As long as I'm with you."

WE PULLED UP TO a concrete building that speared into the sky, with dark glass windows and balconies all along the front. I swear every building in this city looked the same. Rylie got out, tossed the keys to the valet and said, "Please have the items in the trunk brought up."

"Of course, sir."

Rylie held my hand tight as he pulled me into the large foyer. It was all glass walls and rich brown hardwood floors with fancy area rugs I was almost afraid to walk on. The entryway had a chandelier with at least five hundred pieces of glass attached to a black iron frame. It was beautiful, but screamed opulence.

Ferns in large gray concrete pots and a full-sized concrete water display with filigree designs around the base sat below the chandelier. The room itself was easily five times larger than my apartment back in California.

Rylie led me past a few rows of gray leather sofas, one of which had a man who I thought might have been one of the founders of the Watt Millstone factory. I blinked, and he did a double take at me as he read something on his tablet.

We entered the office, where an older, fully gray man rose to his feet and said, "Mr. Allen, what can I do for you?" His eyes flicked to mine and then back to Rylie.

"Frank, do you have the documents I called about earlier? I want Luci to have full rights to anything and everything." Rylie's arm slid around me, and his hand rested on my hip. I felt his thumb move in an attempt to comfort me, but my heart was racing. This place was something that you only saw in movies.

"Of course. I simply need to scan your ID to add to the files." The man named Frank said, looking at me.

"I'm sorry?"

Frank's smile was warm, and I felt Rylie chuckle next to me. "Sweetheart, Frank needs to scan your ID into the system so that the documents can be finalized for you to sign."

"You're putting me on the house?" I said, wide eyed. "Just like that. You are putting me on title to your house. What if I get mad at you and toss you out the window tonight?"

He pulled me close and used a finger to guide my lips to his. "Then I die a happy man. And it's *our* house, sweetheart." His kiss was soft and gentle. "Now sign the fucking paperwork so I can take you upstairs and feed you." My stomach growled again, and I sighed.

I looked down at it and said, "Traitor."

Even Frank chuckled at that. I dug out my wallet, and before I handed my California Driver's License to Frank, I looked at Rylie. "You are sure about this?"

"I've already called my lawyer to get you on the deed, so yes."

"You could still call that off." I said, before Rylie took my ID from my hand and handed it to Frank. "Full access."

"Yes, sir."

Thirty minutes later, I had my own key, programmed in a passcode, and had signed my name so many times, I had lost count. We were in the elevator when he turned to me and said, "I am sorry."

"Rylie. Stop. Seriously. You are going to piss me off if you keep apologizing."

The doors opened to a foyer with a single door. He smiled softly, and took my hand. His hand was clammy and gripped mine tight. Before we got to the door though I asked, "What's wrong?"

"I'm bringing you home for the first time. I'm allowed to be a little nervous, aren't I?"

"There is no reason to be nervous. I am yours, Rylie. I'm not going anywhere."

There was a relieved sigh that came from him as he opened the door and led me inside. I blinked as I took in the space. I wasn't sure what I expected, maybe some immaculate, afraid to touch anything setup that you see in movies, but as I looked around the open area plan, I smiled.

Rylie toed his shoes off and disappeared into the hallway to the left. I took a few steps into the living area and ran my fingers over the soft worn brown leather of the couch. It was cool, and the soft texture soothed my nerves. My attention moved to a fireplace across from the couch that was flanked by two rich brown wooden bookcases. All the shelves were filled with a mix of hardcover and paperback books as well a small collection of DVD's. My eye caught a few of my favorite titles, and my smile grew when I saw Oklahoma. It was my favorite musical, and poor Rylie had watched it countless times with me, even though I knew he found Jud annoying as hell.

Between the fireplace and couch was a brown iron and glass table with a few remotes on it, but I didn't see the TV anywhere. I knew Rylie though, and there was no way he wasn't going to have a TV. I narrowed my eyes, and studied the wall again, looking for the gaming system, and shook my head when I saw it cleverly hidden on the bottom shelf of the bookcase. Proof he was still my Rylie, and there would be a TV somewhere.

As I looked around the condo, I couldn't help but notice how large it was, and while it was about four times the size of my little apartment, it was all things Rylie. Sure, you could tell there was money involved, but it didn't scream billionaire. Not that I knew what that was anymore. I guess I imagined walking in and seeing crystal chandeliers, glass tables, all things white and gray.

Rylie had some of the same furniture that he had before he moved out here. A few pieces I knew were his grandmothers, and I smiled when I saw the painting of Capitola Village on the far wall. It had belonged to his mother and was her most prized possession other than Rylie. It had gutted him when she died.

I turned and looked to where the kitchen was and smiled. Rylie had always been such a whiz in the kitchen, so it didn't surprise me when I saw the stainless steel, professional grade appliances.

"No way, Rye?" I whispered as I went over to the farmhouse style sink, and ran my fingers along the edge. I had always wanted one, and seeing it here, in Rylie's kitchen, did not disappoint. I stood there and admired it for a long moment then became acquainted with what was apparently my new kitchen.

I turned and froze when I looked out the floor to ceiling windows that ran from the dining table at the edge of the kitchen to the corner in the living room. How had I missed this view when I came in?

Rylie came over, and led me to the doors, where he opened one of them. "This is why I stay here. Come here." I followed him out to the deck. Lake Michigan sat before us in all its panoramic glory. For as far as the eye could see there was nothing but the lake.

"It's cold as fuck during the winter months, but it's worth seeing the lake as the ice forms over it."

"Does it freeze over?" I asked, only half aware of the words coming out.

"No, not completely." He wrapped an arm around my waist, pulling me against him, as he slid his hand down the front of my skirt and just let it sit there. It was cool out, and sprinkling, but the difference in temperature was soothing. The lake was a magnificent sight from this high up. God, I was on the 38th floor. My head swam for a minute, but I focused far off in the distance and the feel of him against me.

I leaned back against him and sighed. "I can't believe you live here."

He huffed a laugh and said, "I can't either most days. The Gold Coast is pricey, but when you get views like this... well, it's worth it."

"Harper really gave you all of this?" I said in awe, and Rylie hummed his agreement, then bent down and kissed my neck. I tilted my head to the side and concentrated on the breeze on my face, the feel of his lips against my skin, and how he just held me close to him.

"Come on, let's get you out of those clothes." When I turned to face him, I gave him a knowing smirk. He smiled and said, "I know you can't wait to get into some sweats and a t-shirt."

He led me back inside and down the hall he had gone down earlier where it opened to a room almost the size of my apartment. The bed at the far end was huge. "How... why do you have a bed that huge?"

"It fills the space. It always feels too empty though." He kissed my cheek and said, "Will be better once you're in it."

I rolled my eyes, and he led me to a walk-in closet, where the left side had all his clothes hanging. Suits, dress shirts, dress pants. Shelves that held his jeans, and drawers upon drawers at the far end of the room.

Rylie had already hung all my clothes up and put them away, making the right side look barren. There were three rows of bars which held the dress he had me wear to dinner, and I half wondered when that had been laundered. There were racks and racks for shoes, and a section with drawers at the far end that matched his.

"You are spoiling me, Rylie James."

"Once we move your things from California, we can sort out what else you might need."

"I don't need anything else."

A sad smile fell to his lips as he said, "I won't make you go to all the showboat events, but there will be a few I will ask that you attend, sweetheart." He brushed my hair back from my face, and let the ends curl around his fingers. "So, we will have to get some things. You will hate every minute of it, and I'm sorry for that."

I eyed him, and he said, "First we need to get you moved, though."

"Right away?"

"Preferably. Now, get comfortable and meet me in the kitchen. I'll get some food started."

Chapter Seventeen

I did change, but only into one of his t-shirts. Nothing else. He wanted me to get comfortable, then I would give him a comfortable Luci. I stepped into the master bath and shook my head. The sheer size of everything was going to take some getting used to. There were two full vanity areas, a full glass walk-in shower with dual rain shower heads, and a jacuzzi tub big enough for three people. I smiled knowing we would be taking full advantage of that.

I washed my face and noted some accordion doors opposite the vanity. When I opened them, there was a laundry room with shelves and a full linen closet. I have never understood why laundry rooms had always been off of kitchens. They should always be off bathrooms or bedrooms.

I walked down the carpeted hall and peeked into what ended up being an office and two other bedrooms. Both bedrooms were similarly designed on those gray and white pallets, and were furnished with a gray dresser with drawers, a closet, and a queen bed with a gray headboard and footboard.

When I got to the end of the hall, I leaned against the corner, scanned the condo, if you could even call it that, and watched Rylie cooking over the stove. I had always loved watching him work in the kitchen. I'll never forget the day I came home from a long day with a client in Saratoga, only to find Rylie standing in my kitchen cooking a full meal. He had flown in to surprise me, and decided to cook dinner. He had been oblivious to me walking in that day. I smiled as I heard him humming the same tune he had that night. I inhaled, smelling bacon and when he placed some on the paper towels on the counter, my stomach growled again.

I bit my bottom lip as I watched him. He had taken his shirt off, and his slacks hung low on his hips. Just the hint of his boxers peeked out, and the instant need to wrap my hands around what was impressively rounding out the front of his pants, had me squeezing my legs together. We had done nothing but have sex, but I couldn't get enough of him.

Striding for the kitchen, I snuck up behind him and grabbed a piece of bacon. It was the perfect amount of crunch when I popped it into my mouth.

"HEY!" He said, smacking my hand when I went for another piece.

"What? You are the one starving me and then teasing me with bacon."

"I'm trying to feed your sexy ass." Rylie said, still watching the pan. His eyes flicked over his shoulder and he froze mid-bacon flip. His eyes then trailed from my head to my toes and then back up. I leaned against the counter, slowly chewing on my stolen food, as he said, "You don't play fair."

"What?" I was playing the innocent card, and I heard him groan.

He turned back to the pans, and a minute later, grabbed a plate and loaded it up with eggs and a few slices of bacon. I reached for it, and he held it over my head.

"RUDE!" He looked me up and down and lifted that eyebrow again. He placed the plate down a few feet from me, and then grabbed me by the waist and kissed me. The next thing I knew I was sitting on the counter, and I could feel him hard against me.

"Food, please." I said when he pulled back, his fingers digging into my hips. "Then you can have whatever you want."

The plate now in his hand, he lifted a fork of eggs to my lips and fed me. He waited for me to swallow, and without taking his eyes off mine, he continued to feed me the entire plate of food.

"Aren't you going to eat?" When his gaze fell to my lap, I chuckled and said, "Real food, Rylie. While I thoroughly enjoy when you eat me out, you do need actual food to keep *your* energy up."

I reached over and grabbed another piece of bacon and gave it to him. His fingers dug into my hips again as he lifted the t-shirt.

"Rylie. Please eat. Then you can *eat*." I sighed. "Besides, we need to talk."

His eyes widened only slightly, and I saw that muscle feather in his jaw, when he was nervous about something. He took a deep breath through his nose before saying, "Why does that scare me when you say that? It's never a good sign when your girl says we need to talk."

"Nothing like that." I was looking down at my fingers now, fidgeting with my engagement ring, as he went to make a plate of food for himself. I wasn't second guessing my choice to be with him at all. I waited until I heard him take a bite of food himself, then said, "You said you want me to move in right away?"

"I do." He took another bite and watched me. "Why does that bother you?"

"We... it seems fast." I said, not knowing why I said it.

"It is, considering everything you've learned this weekend. Fuck, just in the last twenty-four hours, but it is the practical decision." He paused for a moment, and said, "If you want your own place here for a while, we can do that. I just know how much you hate moving."

"No. It isn't that."

"Do you want to get a place other than this? Is this too much?" His voice wasn't angry, or anything. All I heard was a man who loved me and wanted to do anything to make me happy. "It's just a condo. We can buy something else. I'm not attached to this one."

"But Harper gave it to you."

"So. If you don't like it, or if it's too much, we can buy something else." He took the last bite of food, and put the plate into the sink. I studied the muscles in his back, and while they bunched and rippled as he moved, he didn't seem angry. Rylie came and stood before me, resting his hands on either side of my hips.

I wasn't sure why I was hesitant to move into this place. It was a dream home. A home I never thought that I could ever afford, let alone want. I turned to look around, and if I were to look for somewhere else, what would I ask for that this place didn't have? What did I need? This place was perfect.

I looked back at Rylie. Just him. That was really all I needed. Just Rylie. I lifted my hand and ran my fingers through the stubble on his jaw. He leaned into the touch. His fingers trailed down my leg and fingered the anklet I wore. A twitch of his lips at the more intimate reason I wore it.

"You would just up and move to another place if I said I didn't like this one?" He blinked like he thought I was crazy for even asking, but I continued, "It's not the house. It's got everything I need."

"Does it have everything you want, though?" He asked, playing with the edge of my shirt.

"It has you."

He leaned forward and kissed me, letting his lips linger on mine for a long moment. "Why the hesitation, Luce? Don't you want to move in with me?" The sound in his voice broke me.

"It's not that at all. It's just a major change, and I'm still trying to absorb it all." I met his gaze and said, "You really want me to move in right away?"

"Yes." There was no hesitation at all. "I've known for months that I don't want to wake another day without you by my side. It took me this long to be able to plan everything out, and then none of it has gone the way it was supposed to."

I smiled at him and said, "You have the next few days off?"

His fingertips ran up my thighs, and I tried to keep from allowing the moan to bubble up, but my back bent toward him and my legs spread further apart in response.

"Theoretically, yes, as long as no other disasters happen at the office." He leaned forward and rested his forehead on mine.

Pulling his hand to the center of me, I tilted my head back and bit my lip as he slowly slid two fingers in me. I whispered, "So, wanna help me pack?"

He froze. "Seriously. You'll move in right now?"

I nodded and begged as I moved my hips toward him, "Please."

He curled his fingers along my front wall, and I whimpered. "I'll give you anything you want."

His fingers threaded through my hair and gripped tight. When his thumb circled my clit, I let out a gush of air and closed my eyes. My hips rolled against him as he finger fucked me on that counter, hitting that delightful spot every time he hooked his fingers.

I was so lost in the pleasure that when he bit down on my nipple I jumped, but a burst of pleasure flowed through me. I tried to look down, but his grip didn't allow me to tilt my head enough to see.

He chuckled and then his hands were on my hips, sliding me off the counter, and lifting his t-shirt I was wearing, up over my head. Only, he tied the shirt around my wrists to keep them together, and turned me around. A soft kiss was placed on my shoulder as he threaded the tee through the handle on the cabinet.

"Rye." I breathed, and when he felt he had my hands adequately taken out of the picture, he lifted my leg, wrapping it around his hip, and in one full stroke, entered me. The coolness of the quartz counter against my nipples, as Rylie pounded into me, had them hardening with each stroke he took.

The sound of our joining filled the kitchen, and I felt his hands gripping my hips. I dug the heel of my foot into him and rolled my hips as he slowed. I lowered my leg, and I felt him run the length of me before slowly re-entering me. I felt myself quiver as he filled me slowly. When he was balls deep, I rolled my hips against him, and his groan flowed over me.

Finally, he reached over and released my hands from the binds of the t-shirt, tossing it to the side. Only, Rylie didn't release me, but grabbed my wrists, and pulled them back behind me, using them as leverage, to thrust into me harder and faster.

"Rylie…" I growled.

"Luci." He moaned, as he pounded into me one last time, releasing himself deep within me. Before I knew what he was doing, I was on my back, heels on the counter, with Rylie diving in. His fingers slid in, and then trailed to my ass, slowly sliding into it. When he slid the second finger into my ass, he clamped down on that bundle of nerves and every muscle in my body tensed as pleasure filled me.

Just as I was coming down, my hand slipped and flipped a switch on the counter next to the sink. A loud grinding sound burst through the room, and it took me half a second longer than Rylie to realize what had happened. His hand was over mine, turning the disposal off.

His eyes met mine. The humor in his eyes cut through the haze, and I started to giggle. "Oops."

"Oops, indeed. At least it wasn't until the end."

"Well, my hands were a bit preoccupied at one point." I said, winking.

"I liked you like that." He pulled me closer and kissed my cheek. I blushed. It wasn't the first time I'd been bound with him. And I always looked forward to exploring new things with him.

His hands rested on my hips, and he pulled me close to him. His forehead rested on mine as he reached up and ran a thumb along my cheek. He cherished me for a long minute before I realized I really had to go to the bathroom.

I rested my arms on his shoulders and kissed him quickly before saying, "I need you to let me down, Rye."

"But, I like you like this."

"And my bladder would really appreciate me relieving it in the appropriate room of the house." I let a mischievous smile cross my lips, and he laughed.

"Alright. Alright. That is one of the few acceptable reasons for you not to be in my arms." He pulled me off the counter and smacked my ass as I turned toward the bathroom. I grabbed the tee before strutting off. I may have let my hips sway a bit more than was necessary.

A low chuckle came from Rylie. "I'll clean up breakfast and meet you on the couch."

"Yes, Rye." I said mockingly.

Chapter Eighteen

The next morning, Rylie walked around the corner as I stepped out of the bathroom. "I just got off the phone. We leave in two hours."

"You were able to arrange for a flight that quick?" I shook my head, a small smile lifting the side of my mouth. "Of course, you did."

"You'll be flying first class, sweetheart. Every step of the way from here to eternity." He kissed my temple and then slapped my ass.

"What no private corporate jets?" I teased.

Rylie shrugged and said, "They are spoken for, and I don't really like them anyways. Feels like I'm flaunting the money." He wrinkled his nose and it was adorable on him. "So, I usually travel commercially, but splurge on first-class seats. They are just squishier, and more comfortable."

I laughed at that as I got dressed. It was such a Rylie answer. "You know I was only joking about the private jet thing, right?"

"I know, but I really don't feel right using the money I kind of fell into like that. Sure, I've worked my ass off this last year to keep it going, and have had to learn everything about running this company, but I also realize I've been lucky to have excellent advisors." He was buttoning his shirt, when he faced me and continued, "Like I've been saying, Luci, while the company and money are a lot of work, its also a lot of image and bullshit."

"I know, Rye. You are still that same kid I grew up with, and you are still the same man you were when you moved out here. The same man that Harper believed was worthy enough to hand you everything." I rested my hand on his heart, and said, "That is the man I fell in love with. That is the man I am choosing to marry."

Then as I palmed him and he ground against my hand, I said, "Doesn't mean I am not going to tease you for it." I looked down and ran a single finger along the length of him as I pulled my hand away. There would be no way to make that flight if I didn't, and whispered, "And you are insatiable."

"Only for you, sweetheart."

EIGHT HOURS LATER, WE picked up the rental car at the San Jose Airport and headed off to pack up my apartment. I had called Katie and asked her to drop off some packing boxes at the house so I could start right away. She said they would be there before I got home, and that she would be over tomorrow to help pack. My phone buzzed, and I didn't recognize the number.

Opening the messages, I paused, reading through the string.

Unknown:

Hey baby doll. When you coming home from Mr. Moneybags? Hurry back to my arms. I'll remind you what a real man is like.

You know the rules. Why haven't you answered yet?

I'm trying to be a patient man, baby doll.

That's three messages you haven't responded to. You know the punishment for that, too.

Lucille. Answer me.

I'm waiting.

"What's wrong?" Rylie said, reaching over and resting his hand on my thigh.

"Asshole just broke the restraining order and has my new number." I screenshotted the messages, and texted the lawyer so he could would have them for his file.

"You are sure they are from Justin?"

I turned the phone so he could see when we stopped at the light. "He's the only one who ever called me baby doll. He had this rule, that I had to text him back within five minutes, or I would get punished."

Rylie's hand gripped tighter. "He got served the paperwork shortly after BMT refused to run with his statements. I'm not surprised he's pissed, but how did he get your new number?"

I shrugged. "There's any number of ways. I use it so much for work, he could have impersonated a client."

His fingers tightened on my thigh again as he looked at me while we were at the stoplight. "You, okay?"

Surprisingly, I was. "I know I freaked out at your office, and I'm sorry for that, but…" I knitted my eyebrows together, took a deep breath and said, "I am okay. I don't know why, but I'm really okay. It might have something to do with you being with me."

The light turned green, and Rylie hesitated for only a moment, before continuing onto the apartment. I stared out the window as I watched the storefronts, and life I was leaving behind, stream by.

The minutes went by in silence, and Rylie continued to study me each time we stopped. When we got to the light before we would turn into the gated community, I turned to him, squeezing his hand on my leg saying, "Seriously, Rye, I'm okay. It's just another reason why I should move in with you, immediately. Your place has more security, and I'll be further from him."

"He found out you were in the Bay Area, though. When you moved from Sac, I thought you would be able to hide better amongst the people from him. We all did."

"Sacramento isn't all that far though, Rylie. A day trip would be easy for Justin. Besides, it's not that hard to find someone."

"Not my point. When he put you in the hospital… I almost couldn't handle it. Then you got that restraining order, it gave me, all of us, peace of mind. I know it's only a piece of paper, but you started going to the range again, and… Then you moved. You were going to be closer to Katie, closer to most of our friends…"

"I can't live in fear." I said to myself more as a mantra than something I accepted. I knew I couldn't live in fear, but… "Healing is hard."

"It is, but I'm a bit scared by the difference between yesterday and today's reactions."

"I wasn't anticipating him showing his cards that quickly yesterday." I kissed him quickly before the light turned green, and said, "Now today, and these texts? I'm surprised he has the number, but the fact he tried to reach out after you so gloriously shut down his plan to…" I waved my hand in the air, "Do whatever it was he was planning? No. That doesn't surprise me."

Rylie shook his head, as he turned into the entrance to the complex, and entered my access code for the gate to open. There was a spot close to the walkway, and as we got out of the car, he took my hand and squeezed it hard.

"The sooner you are moved in, the better I'll feel."

I pulled him to a stop and kissed him on the cheek. He was worried about Justin, but they were only texts. "That's what we are here for."

I got to the gate to my building, and punched in the code. I changed it every couple of months to ensure that even if Justin ever got it, he wouldn't be able to get in. Once through, we walked down the brick walkway to my door. I turned the key in the lock, threw my keys into the bowl by the door, and flipped the light on. Rylie had me behind him and against the door a second later.

CHAPTER NINETEEN

"Rylie." I muttered.

"Just me, you, and Katie have a key, right?"

"Yes." I drawled, and then looked around Rylie's shoulder to see that my living room was completely wrecked. I blinked when I saw my apartment. Furniture was tossed, drawers thrown open, papers strewn all over the brown carpet. I looked to my bedroom, where my bedding had been stripped and thrown to the side, and even the mattress was halfway off the box spring. My clothes were thrown in every direction, including my underwear drawer completely dumped out right at the doorway.

I looked toward my kitchen and there was a picture of Rylie on the wall, where someone had taken each of my kitchen knives using his face for target practice.

I quickly grabbed Rylie's phone from his back pocket and called 911. I turned the sound down, and when I vaguely heard them answer, I rattled off the address. "Someone has broken into my apartment and trashed it."

My eyes went to where I kept my gun in it's safe as Rylie said, "Stay in here. I'll check the rest of the apartment."

I nodded to him as the 911 operator asked me if there were any weapons in the house. "Yes. I have a Springfield 9mm. Registered."

"Thank you, ma'am. Is it secured in the home?" The voice said on the other end of the line.

I froze when I heard Rylie say, "Justin, how did you get in here?"

I heard the dispatcher try to ask a few questions, but I couldn't turn the volume up for fear that Justin would hear.

"Rylie Allen." Justin slurred.

I strode to the safe, and when I opened it, I whispered, "My gun is gone, and my ex-boyfriend, who I have a restraining order on, is in my apartment. My fiance, Rylie Allen, just found him in the bedroom. Please get the police here now."

A shot rang through the air, and I ran toward the bedroom, where I found Rylie and Justin tangled in a mess of legs and arms. The sound of crunching and snapping was quickly followed by Justin screaming. Rylie reached back and his fist swung, hitting Justin square in the nose. The impact sent my crazy ex off the bed and crashing onto the floor.

When he didn't move, I ran to Rylie's side, tripped over the coffee table, and crashing into myself on the doorjamb. "Are you okay?"

"I'm fine. The shot went wide." He gathered me in his arms and pulled me back into the living room.

"Where is my gun, Rylie?" I asked carefully.

"I don't know. Probably fell under the bed." Rylie's attention went to a spot on my forehead, and shook his head. "How did you get hurt?"

"What?"

"You are bleeding," he wiped a spot on my temple and I crunched my eyebrows in confusion.

"I have no idea." I shook my head. "Seriously. I'm fine. I would feel a lot better if I had my Springfield in my hand right now. Where is it?"

"Looking for this?" Justin said, waving it in the air and wiping his nose. He was leaning against my bedroom doorjamb, before pushing off the frame and limping into the living room.

Rylie pulled me behind him as I found the strength to say, "Justin, you are breaking the restraining order by being here. You have destroyed my apartment, and I want you to leave."

"OH, but Luci, that restraining order is just a piece of paper show... showing how much I... how much I love you." Justin slurred, taking a few more limping steps into the living room. Rylie was trying to get me closer to the front door, but stopped when Justin said, "You are mine Luci. Always have, always will."

"You lost me when you beat me and I spent four days in the hospital." My hands balled into fists, to keep the shaking under control.

"That was an unfortunate event. Unfortunate indeed." He said, nodding his head, but sighed. "One that I hope doesn't happen again."

I saw lights flashing through the window in the kitchen, but kept my eyes trained on Justin. He waved my gun around his head. "That restraining order and this gun don't do you any good if you don't have them. It takes the police an average of what, ten minutes to respond? If you even have a chance to notify them?"

I knew officers in the San Jose Police Department. I knew that time was closer to five to eight minutes. I flicked my eyes to the clock on the wall, and it had been seven minutes since that call first went through.

"Justin, please put the gun down." I didn't care if I sounded like I was begging. I knew I was begging. He smiled then.

"You are so protective of her, Rylie." Justin said and huffed a laugh. "I wanted to try to talk some reason into you at the restaurant the other night, but there were so many guards pushing the media back, I couldn't get close."

I froze, and forced myself to breathe. I hadn't been seeing things.

"What were you even doing in Chicago, Justin?" Rylie said through his teeth.

Justin shrugged, but winced at the movement. "I always watch over my baby doll."

I thought I had heard someone in the hallway, and even Justin's eyes flickered to the door, but then he just cocked his head to the side and said, "There is no one to help the all-mighty, Rylie Allen now. Your money and influence can't stop me here."

"Justin put the gun down. I'll let you leave. No one has to get hurt here today. Please just leave." Tears streamed down my face, and I gripped the back of Rylie's shirt. I would never forgive myself if Rylie got hurt. I would pull him back behind me if Justin raised that gun.

Rylie's arm was still in front of me and on my hip. Justin turned to face me and said, "You wouldn't come back with me, would you?"

"Justin. Please, put the gun down and we will talk this out. No one needs to get hurt." Rylie's voice was even, and one that I'm sure he used in many a board meeting. He was trying to get us out of here, but I could see the crazed look in Justin's eye. See the hatred for him on his face that said he wanted Rylie out of the way.

A cruel, sinister chuckle came from him as he said to Rylie, "Rylie Allen, the almighty. The untouchable." His eyes flicked to me quickly, before going back to Rylie. "You have her wrapped around your little finger, don't you?"

"More like I'm wrapped around hers." Rylie said, lifting his head. "Please put the gun down, Justin."

"No." Justin took a step toward Rylie and shouted at him, spreading his arms wide, "You ruined me. You ruined my life. I needed that money from BMT to pay off my debts."

"I don't give a shit about your money problems, Justin. That isn't Luci nor my problem. I'm only trying to protect Luci."

"Justin, please stop." I begged again, taking a step back.

"You ruined me!" Justin's voice was eerily calm as he turned that gun toward me. "Now I'll ruin you. If she won't be mine, then neither of us can have her."

I stared down the barrel of my own gun and I knew Justin would pull that trigger, so I looked to Rylie and mouthed, 'I love you' and waited for the gun to go off.

In the span of seconds, Rylie lunged forward just as a gunshot rang through the air, but I felt nothing. Out of the corner of my eye, I saw Justin fall to the ground, and before I knew it, I was wrapped up in Rylie's arms.

There was a flurry of motion happening around us as I stared at Justin, who turned his head toward me and smiled. There was a brief flicker of sadness in his eyes before he was staring into the unknown. His chest stopped moving, and then there was nothing.

Rylie turned to look back at him. "Shit."

He pulled me into the bedroom and then up into his lap. He rocked me back and forth, saying, "It's okay, sweetheart. Everything is okay."

I turned and wrapped my legs around his hips and my arms around his neck, trembling and clinging to him. His arms wrapped tightly around my waist, and I muttered into his neck, "You okay? You're not hurt?"

"I'm fine, sweetheart. You okay?"

I nodded my head and held him tighter. The bedroom door shut behind me as an officer introduced himself and his partner. I didn't hear their names. I was just replaying Justin dying before me.

"Mr. Allen, we need to speak to Ms. Baker. Can we do that, please?"

"Luci. They need to talk to you, and you at least turn around so they can hear you?"

"Rylie."

"I'm fine, sweetheart. Fists are going to be a little sore, but I'm okay." I loosened my grip on him, and he helped me reposition myself on his lap.

"Can I speak to you alone, Ms. Baker?" The taller one said.

"No." My voice was hard, and my grip on Rylie's hand on my knee became firmer. I turned to look him over, and only saw a few scrapes and a cut on his temple, but I asked again, "You hurt?"

"I'm fine, sweetheart. Please talk to the police." He kissed my temple and nodded to the officers standing in my bedroom.

"We need to get your statements." The shorter one said.

"It was all on the 911 call." Rylie said carefully. "Pull the recording."

"That is true, however, we only have audio, and some of it was muffled. We need more details of what happened."

I took a deep breath and let it out slowly. "My ex broke into my house, thrashed it, somehow got my gun out of the safe, fought my fiance, and threatened to kill him in front of me, and then pointed the gun at me to kill me." I said, and then a fog lifted from my head. My heart started to slow, and I looked at Rylie, tears streaming down my face. "He was going to kill you, Rye."

"No, he was going to kill you." He said, kissing me on the temple again. There was so much pain in his voice that when I looked at the cops again, I asked, "What more do you need? You know what happened after that.

Someone else shot and killed him. It wasn't Rylie or I. Who did that?"

"When we broke through the door, one of the other officers... diffused the situation."

"If you think I'm sorry for that, think again." I snapped. "I had a restraining order on Justin Devereaux for a reason. I bought the Springfield for my own personal protection because of Justin Devereaux. I don't care if it makes me look bad, because I'm not sorry that piece of shit is dead."

The officer blinked and nodded his head before saying, "Do you have somewhere you can stay tonight?"

"I was planning on staying in my apartment, but now that it is a crime scene..."

Rylie finished for me as I trailed off. "I'll find us a hotel to stay in tonight. We were only here to pack things up and get them ready for her move to Chicago."

"Everything is sold out locally. Between the concert, the Giants game with the Dodgers, and the festival at the fairgrounds, you might not get anything on this short notice."

"I'll work on it." Rylie said.

"You mentioned going to Chicago? We won't be able to allow you to leave the state till this is settled." The shorter cop said.

"It's not likely we could flee anywhere without the media knowing about it." I said, "I'll give you my cell number. I'll give you a fucking confirmation code, whatever it is that you need to get patched through—"

"Sweetheart, stop." Rylie said, turning my face to look at him. Those gray eyes met mine with a new, determined focus. "He is just doing his job. He knows that we aren't a flight risk. He also knows he will be able to get a hold of me, whether we are here or in Chicago." His face turned hard as he faced the cop, and said, "Isn't that right, officer?"

"I'm sure that is the case, Mr. Allen, however —"

"I need to be somewhere safe, and that is back in my own home in Chicago. I don't feel safe here." I hissed through my teeth. Rylie's eyes didn't leave mine, and there was understanding there. I was freaking out and trying to put on a front. I was scared, and I had just watched my ex try to kill not only me but also him. Then I watched him die.

"Who else do you feel you are in danger of? Mr. Devereaux is deceased. He can't hurt you." The taller one said.

I blinked. I could do nothing but blink. Rylie simply said, "My fiance and I refuse to say anything else until we have had a chance to talk to our lawyer. If you wouldn't mind, please step out of the room, so we can do so."

The cops looked at me and I nodded. I wasn't lying. Once the media knew that Rylie and I were involved in a domestic incident, it would be mayhem. I wanted to get back to Chicago and hole up in the condo as soon as possible.

With a heavy sigh, they left and Rylie pulled out his phone, hit a few buttons. After a long conversation, I only understood bits and pieces of, hung up the phone, and said, "Pack anything you want to take with you right away. Once they clear the scene, I'll have movers come and move whatever is left."

A knot released in my chest as it registered. Rylie would take care of everything. I wrapped my arms around his waist and said, "I know I tease you about the money and everything, but this, this is why I love you. You know how to handle me when I'm freaking out. You just take charge and handle me." He kissed the top of my head and sighed.

"I almost lost you today, sweetheart." The sound of his voice breaking with that statement had me looking up at him, and I couldn't help but reach up and wipe the tears from his cheeks. "I never want to feel that kind of fear again. I will do everything I can to protect you. I would go through hell itself to keep you safe, and I very well may burn in the depths of hell should anyone hurt a hair on that pretty little head of yours."

I felt the honest truth in those words. I reached up on my toes and kissed him softly. He didn't release me though, he just pulled me up and kissed me harder. It was a deep claiming kiss. One of fear. One of passion, and one of love.

There was a knock on the door, and the cop came back in to say, "We will need to talk to you again in the morning, and then you should be able to head back to Chicago."

Rylie's phone vibrated in his hand, and it was only then I realized he had it. "How did you get your phone?"

He smirked at me and said, "I grabbed it as I pulled you in here." He looked at the message and then turned to the taller cop and said, "We will be staying at The Glamin on Santana Row."

He reached into his back pocket though and pulled his wallet out, went to my makeshift desk and wrote something on the back of the card, before handing it to him. "That number gets out, I'll know where it came from. Do not compromise our safety and your ability to investigate this case."

The cop blinked and nodded. "I'm assuming it would be better for us to come to you in the morning?"

"Plain clothes will be best. I'd like the media not to get a hold of this. It's obvious from the 911 call, our statements, your statements, and the body cam footage, what really happened here today. Oh, and Luci's security code access to the security camera footage, is 0825. I'm sure that will provide you with whatever other evidence you may need. Copies of it are uploaded every ten minutes to a secure offsite location, so I will know if any of it is tampered with. I'm not in any legal trouble, but my lawyer will meet us in the morning. Meet us around 10am? He's taking a red eye."

Chapter Twenty

After we checked into the hotel, I cleaned Rylie's knuckles and the cut on his temple. He had a few other scratches on him, but I was grateful he was still standing before me. The entire time I cleaned him up, his hands never left my hips. When I was finished, I kissed his forehead, stripped to nothing, and crawled into bed.

Rylie changed his clothes, crawled in behind me, and laid there holding me, as my mind started replaying everything that happened. Justin had gotten through security, into my apartment without damaging the door, and then into my safe. How had he even done that? I felt my breathing quicken, and my heart started to race.

"Shhh, sweetheart. I've got you. You're safe." Rylie whispered in my ear, and turned me to face him. He kissed my forehead and pulled me closer.

"Even with all the security... all the precautions we have taken in regard to my safety in that apartment, Rylie... Justin got in. Justin was trying to take me back by force." I gripped onto his t-shirt he had changed into, and looked up at him. "He pointed the gun at us. He would have pulled the trigger, too. I saw it in his eyes. He would have done it if the police hadn't gotten there exactly when they did."

Rylie's chest shuddered slightly, but a moment later his voice was steady in my ear as he said, "I know. I keep replaying it in my head. I can't figure out how he got in. You changed the code recently to the gate, right?"

"Just last week."

"I'll get copies of the security footage and see what we can find so that it doesn't happen again." He squeezed me and his voice was strained again, "I installed the best Webster Enterprises could give you. We market it for domestic violence victims. We have to do better. I almost lost you."

"We almost lost each other." I kissed the hollow of his throat, and he rolled on top of me. He studied me for a long moment before leaning down and giving me a soft, lingering kiss.

"I won't wrap you in bubble wrap, but I will do everything I can to prevent this from happening again." I nodded, and my stomach growled. He leaned down and kissed my nose. "In the meantime, I'll order food."

"Chicken Ceaser salad if they have one, please." When he tilted his head to the side in question, I just said, "I don't want anything too heavy."

He nodded, and ordered. When it came, Rylie handed me a t-shirt and answered the door. I watched as he set the table so we could sit and eat. "What?" He asked with a smile.

I shook my head and smiled, "Just... You are doting on me, and I don't know how to feel about it."

"Get used to it, Mrs. Allen." He said as he came to stand before me, bent down and gave me a small kiss. Then he took me by the hand and had me sitting at the table. "Now come and eat."

We were watching a trivia game show, but the news interrupted and cut to a scene where a blonde was standing in front of my apartment building.

"Rylie." I said carefully, and when I pointed to the TV, he turned it up a notch to the blonde saying, "Reports say that there was a disturbance at Webster Enterprises CEO's fiance's apartment earlier today. San Jose PD is saying that there is a deceased individual, but no further information has been released yet."

Rylie's eyes met mine, and I shook my head, as I popped a piece of the roll that came with our dinner into my mouth. It was buttery and practically melted on my tongue. "Just a piece of shit who doesn't deserve a grave."

Rylie blinked at me and sat up straighter.

"What? Tell me I'm wrong?"

"I mean you're not, but... Luce, that's harsh, even for you." He said, shaking his head. "I wish he hadn't passed out that quick. I only got in a couple of good punches."

He flexed his hands, and the skin split again where he had made contact with Justin's nose.

WHEN WE WOKE THE next morning, Rylie was holding me tight against him. I had woken on and off throughout the night and had seen him awake every time. He had just kissed me softly on the temple or the top of my head, told me he loved me, until I fell back asleep.

I rolled over and put my hand over his heart. Rylie had hardly slept. The shadows under his eyes were dark, and I wasn't so sure that one of them wasn't a black eye. "Rye, I know you are not okay. I don't expect you to be. It's okay to admit it."

His mouth opened, then closed, then opened again, before he let out a long breath. "I almost lost you."

"You didn't."

"But—"

"You didn't." I kissed him and then said, "And if I had died, it would not have been your fault. You did everything you could. But, I didn't die. I am lying here in your arms, feeling safe, because of you."

"I can't lose you, sweetheart." A tear fell down his cheek, and I smiled at him.

"You aren't going to. My biggest problem isn't a problem anymore. May he rot in the deepest depths of hell, too."

He kissed me, and it was soft and sweet. I held onto him for a long minute before the alarm went off on my phone. I growled as I rolled over and turned it off. "Fucking thing. Always ruining my fun."

I crawled out of bed, and when he laid there, watching me, I let my gaze go down his form, and back up to meet his eyes. "Come shower with me."

His eyes widened slightly. "Don't have to ask me twice."

The bed bounced as he launched himself off of it and I ran toward the bathroom, Rylie quick on my heels. When I got to the door, I blocked it and it was only then that his eyes heated. Smirking, I turned to get the water started, and when I leaned over, he pressed his glorious cock against my ass.

I turned, and before he knew what was happening, I was on my knees and taking him into my mouth, licking, and sucking as I slipped his pants to the floor and he stepped out, kicking them to the hall. I didn't wait for any reaction as I released him and hummed against his balls.

"Jesus woman." He said, thrusting himself down my throat over and over again. His moans echoed in the tiled bathroom, and I reached down to finger myself.

The room was filling with steam when he lifted me from the ground and kissed me, carrying me into the shower. "You are good at your distractions."

I smiled against his lips. "It's easy to do when I have you."

He set me down, and when I stood under the hot water, he let his hands linger over my skin, which did nothing but make me hot and cold in all the right places. When he noticed my nipples harden, he chuckled and moved to rinse the shampoo from his hair. I took the opportunity to grind my ass against him. There was a throaty chuckle as he grabbed my hips and thrust into me.

I braced myself against the wall, and bowed my back to allow him more access, and just moaned out, "Rylie, fuck me. Please, just fuck me hard."

The sound of our skin slapping against each other and my cries of pleasure at him pounding into me filled the room. I didn't even remotely try to keep it quiet. So much had happened this weekend. All I wanted was to get lost in Rylie.

When I reached down and started rubbing my clit, Rylie bit into my shoulder, slamming harder into me. His grip on my hips was so tight it hurt. Each burst of pain sent pleasure through me at the thought that it was because he was claiming me as his, and losing himself in his own primal needs. God. It was enough to make me fall for him all over again.

"Fuck, Luci!" He screamed as he released himself into me. He slowed, and then dropped to his knees, lifting a leg over his shoulder and clamped down on my clit. My arms flung out to either side of the shower to brace myself. He took my weight and slid three fingers into me as he lapped, sucked, and nibbled on my clit until I couldn't hold it back anymore. I exploded, screaming into the world.

When he stood, he held me close and kissed me. I wrapped my arms around his shoulders as his tongue ran the length of my lips, and I opened for him. His tongue danced across mine, and I reveled in the taste of our mixed release on his lips.

He pulled back and smiled. "I love your distractions."

"Any time, Rylie. Glad to be of service." He kissed me quickly again, and said, "Okay, let's finish up and get dressed. Joseph Feldspar and the officers will be here shortly."

"Who is Feldspar?"

"Our personal lawyer, sweetheart. He's bringing some other documents for you to sign after when we are done with San Jose's finest."

I eyed him carefully. "I'm not going to like this, am I?"

"Probably not, but you're going to sign them and love me forever." He slapped my ass before saying, "Now go get dressed. I don't want anyone else seeing what's mine naked."

Hum. I reached for the anklet on the counter, and said, "We should solidify what all this anklet is going to mean."

Rylie secured the towel around his waist, and came behind me. He took the anklet from my hand, and kneeled down, securing it back on my ankle. He played with it a bit before looking up at me, water still clinging to his eyelashes as he said, "It will mean whatever you want it to mean. That anklet and ring on your finger both signify that I will love and take care of you eternally. We don't have time now to iron out all the details, but when we get home, we will have that conversation."

I could accept that, so I just nodded and got dressed. When there was a knock on the door, I sat in the oversized grey chair in the corner and brought my knees to my chest.

Rylie had a conversation with a man who was maybe five feet ten and almost white blond hair, who came in and settled into one of the chairs at the table, and Rylie said, "Luci, sweetheart. This is Joe. I'll be saving his information on your phone."

I gave him an even look, and he just smiled at me as he raised his eyebrow at me.

"Hello, Joe."

"Nice to meet you, Ms. Baker."

Joe and Rylie then immediately went into a barrage of legal talk about what happened yesterday. When the officers came in, I rehashed what had happened, and the entire time Rylie didn't let go of my hand. When they were done, we were told we could go home, but to please answer any phone calls that come from the Department.

"Of course." I mumbled.

Joe showed them out and then came to sit down in front of us. "Now, to the other matters."

I narrowed my eyes at Rylie, who just beamed at me.

"Mr. Allen, I have made the changes to the trust documents. Have you had a chance to review them?"

"I have, and they are accurate." Rylie's eyes hadn't left mine.

"Sign where these are tabbed, then."

Rylie got to the last page and smiled. "This is where you need to sign."

"Why am I signing anything on your trust?" I leaned over and looked at the document he had just finished scribbling his name to. When I read the first few lines, I cursed. "Rylie James Allen."

"I take it he didn't warn you he was naming you as the sole beneficiary of the trust, and adding you as the Trustee, in all his personal affairs."

"No. He just told me I would be signing a bunch of things, and that I would then be loving him forever. Which I will do whether I sign this shit or not."

"Sweetheart, you're going to be my wife. You will already receive everything anyway. I'm not having you sign a prenup, because none of this will matter if I don't have you. If it has my name on it, it's yours as well. I don't want there to be a question about it, should something happen to me."

"Is this in response to yesterday?"

"No. Rylie had me draw up these documents over a month ago." Joe interjected and then looked between us.

"You get everything." Rylie said again.

"Maybe after we are married!" I said incredulously. "What if, over the next six months of living with me, you decide I'm not good enough for your life? What if you find out you don't love me, but only the image that was cultivated between our previous relationship?"

He looked at me, unflinching, and said, "You still get everything."

"Rylie..." I breathed his name, and he had nothing but love and adoration in his eyes. I also saw that fierce determination that told me he wasn't going to back down on this.

"Give me a minute. I'm not signing shit until I know exactly what I'm putting my name down for."

I started reading through the documents, and Rylie's sizeable list of assets, as well as all the legal jargon that came with it. I knew Harper had left him a lot of large accounts on the personal side of things, but when I saw the estimated value as of a week ago, I slide the paperwork back across the table, and said "There is an error on the estimation of worth page."

Joe took the document and checked the numbers again over the next twenty minutes, and when he was done, he made some pen and ink changes before handing it back to me. "Good eye, Ms. Baker. Here are the corrected amounts."

"You just changed them to be higher. There are too many zeros in that number." I pulled on the years of professionalism to keep the astonishment out of my voice.

"No ma'am. These are the correct figures." My heart stopped. I completely froze. I knew he was rich, but holy shit. I looked up at him, then to the lawyer, and then to the paperwork again. No. There was a mistake.

"No. Rylie's worth is tied up in Webster Enterprises." I looked at Rylie, whose smile stretched from ear to ear. I looked between them and a sly smile crossed Joe's face.

"She really had no idea how dripping in diamonds she was about to become, did she?" Joe said, chuckling at Rylie.

"Nope." Rylie said with a pop of his lips.

"How did you keep this from her?" Joe said to Rylie, who shrugged.

"She's never cared about money. I knew she loved me for me. When we are here in California, I've just been Rylie. In Chicago, we hid away." Rylie came to crouch in front of me and took my head in my hands. "None of it means anything to me. I have you, and you are my most prized possession."

"Rye..." Tears fell down my cheeks, and he kissed them away.

"Please, just sign the documents." I nodded and then went to signing my name in about fifty different places. Apparently, Rylie was also changing the name of the Trust to. 'Rylie and Luci Allen's Family Trust'. So, there were six or seven deeds that had to be signed for my name to be added to them, not including the transfers for all the stocks, and bank accounts, both in the US and offshore. Then there were the transfers of property in a few cities here in the states, but there were also the international properties in Australia, New Zealand, China, France, England, and even a small island off the coast of Ecuador. I couldn't believe the amount of property that there was.

When we finished, I sat there, stunned. I was staring at the stack of paperwork as Rylie signed a bunch of other stuff with Joe. Harper had set up Rylie for generations if everyone was smart. I looked up at him as he was talking about some acquisition in Kentucky, and he smiled at me softly. I returned it, but looked back at the stack of documents on the table.

My fingers tapped the table, as I looked out the window trying to absorb how my whole life had taken a turn that I couldn't even say it had taken a 180. It had gone so far beyond that; I felt like it had taken a 540. When I left my apartment a few days ago, I was just Lucille Baker, Project Designer for Kovinal Engineers and Designs. Granted, Luci had a boyfriend, and a crazy ex, but who didn't have a crazy ex in their life. Now, I was engaged to my boyfriend, who was a freaking billionaire, and I had signed the documents to add my name to all those assets. Not to even mention the reason why we were sitting in this hotel room.

The sun parted from the clouds just then and I smiled. Justin couldn't bother me ever again. He was gone. I felt a weight lift off my chest. I leaned back in the chair and instantly felt the exhaustion settle over me.

A nap. I needed a nap. Rylie and Joe were halfway through a discussion when I just got up and laid down on the bed.

Chapter Twenty-One

I woke up to Rylie stroking my hair and saying, "Come on, sweetheart. Let's go home. Then we can sleep for days."

I nodded, and in a daze over all that had occurred this weekend, let him take me to the airport. We were sitting in the terminal when one of the news stations in the bar next to where we were sitting caught my eye.

"Justin Devereaux was shot and killed by police yesterday when he tried to kill Webster Enterprise's CEO, Rylie Allen and his fiance. No one is talking from the Allen camp yet, but reports say Allen and his fiance are unharmed. Lucille Baker had a restraining order filed against Devereaux after Devereaux attacked her and inflicting injuries that sent her the hospital."

"Rye." I said, grabbing his arm. He looked up and read the last portion of the closed-circuit text and said, "Shit."

Grabbing my hand, he dragged me straight to the security office. I was glad Justin was gone, but the events of yesterday had that deep-seated terror rushing to the surface. I had flashbacks of Justin pointing my own gun at me and started shaking again.

Rylie was asking for a private entrance to the plane, and when they said that there wasn't a way for them to do that this close to boarding, they offered to have us board last, and would start boarding now. Once they had boarded the rest of the plane, they closed off first class and allowed us to board.

I had no concept of time, but I couldn't stop shaking. He muttered something to the stewards of the plane, and then a few minutes later, they came back with two small shot glasses.

"Drink." Rylie said.

"I didn't think you could drink on the planes anymore." He raised an eyebrow, and I was shocked. "Did you actually pull the Rylie Allen card?"

"When it suits my purpose, I do use it." He smirked. "It will get me nowhere with you, but drink."

"Rylie. I'm not sure—"

"Sweetheart, you haven't stopped shaking since you saw that newsreel. I have two shots. Now. Drink."

I sighed. He was right, of course. I took the first and let the warm liquid coat my throat and reached for the second immediately, letting the first burn heighten the taste of the first.

"Now hopefully you will relax some." He put his arm around my shoulder and pulled me close to him.

The pilot came on and gave their normal disclosures and statements, and said, "We will be next for take-off."

I looked around and only just then noticed that there wasn't anyone else sitting with us. "Rylie, did you buy out first class?"

He smiled and kissed my temple as he pulled me to him. "Last night. I paid off the other four seats that had been sold, and pulled some strings with the airline."

I nodded, and then he chuckled before saying, "I called to see how soon one of the company jets could be here, but it wasn't going to be available tonight, and I knew you'd want to get back home as soon as possible."

I chuckled. "I do. I want to leave everything in California behind me."

"Everything?" He asked, running his hand up and down my arm.

"Not you or Katie, but I want to leave all the bad stuff." I sighed heavily as the airplane sped down the runway and lifted off the ground. I sat straight up. "Katie! I didn't call Katie. She's probably freaking out right now." I fumbled for my phone, but then realized that it wasn't going to work now that we were in the air.

"It's okay. I called her after I was done with Joe, while you were sleeping. She wants you to check in with her tomorrow, though, okay?"

I nodded and chewed on my thumb. There has been so much that has been happening in the last few days. My life has completely changed. I should be panicking, but... I wasn't. I had Rylie. Justin was gone. Forever.

"What are you thinking, sweetheart?"

"Just how much things have changed in a few days." I leaned back to look at him and twisted in my seat. "My ex tried to kill me, and the man I love. Who also happened to tell me he is a billionaire, and not just any billionaire, but the CEO of Webster Enterprises."

He smiled, but there was something in his eyes, not shined, but dulled all at the same time. "And I got engaged to that man. I'm freaking getting married, Rye!"

"I'm aware, sweetheart, and damn if it doesn't make me a jealous man. I should do something about that." I gave him a look as the plane banked, and I felt the alcohol hit my head. "Oh right, I'm the lucky bastard."

I smiled, pulled my sweater tighter around me, and leaned my head on his shoulder as the plane evened out. "Sleep sweetheart. I'll be here to watch over you."

I WOKE UP TO the plane descending and Rylie rubbing the sleep from his eyes. I smiled at him. "I'm glad to see you got some sleep, too."

"Yea, I guess I did. Sorry. Guess I wasn't watching over you." I kissed him on the cheek, just as the wheels touched down.

When we landed, the pilot said, "If everyone could, please stay in their seats for the time being." I looked at him and gave him a questioning look, that he just shrugged at.

The steward came over and said, "Mr. and Mrs. Allen, we will stop in a moment to allow you to disembark.

We will then let the rest of the passengers off at the standard gate."

"Can you even do that?" I asked. Even Rylie shrugged at that one.

The plane came to a stop, and I grabbed my work bag. Rylie grabbed his duffle and the two carry-on bags that had pretty much the only things I had to have from the apartment. If everything else got lost in between California and here, I would be disappointed, but not devastated. The only exception to that would be the bookshelf my grandfather had made when I was a kid.

Once we were stopped, and the ladder had been put into place, the door opened and Rylie took my hand and led me out. It was cold enough that I could see my breath as we stepped outside, and I wish I had my jacket. We made our way down to where a limo was waiting for us. I gave him a roll of my eyes, and he just tipped his head back and laughed.

I slid into the seat, and when Rylie sat down next to me, he pulled a fleece blanket from one of the compartments, laid it over my lap, and rubbed my arms.

"I'm not used to all this special treatment, Rylie." Tears leaked, and I felt one plop on my shirt. At this point, I didn't know how to process all the emotions that were going through me.

"It's okay, sweetheart. It takes some getting used to. When it comes to you, though, I'm going to use that privilege. If it had just been me traveling, I would have sat in first-class, but I would have sat there with all the other saps, and boarded and unboarded just like everyone else."

I shook my head and said, "Under normal circumstances, I want it to be that way. I am not going to lie. First-class is more comfortable, but I don't know about all the extra special treatment. On a normal trip. Right now, I just want to get home."

After a few minutes, the car was on the highway, taking us back to the condo.

"When I learned I could hide by going commercial, and it made it harder for the media to get pictures, I started taking those flights. They look for the special treatment. However, with what happened in California, I am thankful for the special treatment, because not one camera was seen. I want to hold off having you in front of the cameras for a few days."

"What about a formal engagement announcement?" I asked carefully.

"Do you want to do one? I didn't think you would. I hadn't even thought about it being a thing." He said, taking my hand and running his thumb over the ring again.

"Wouldn't it be expected for us to go through all the high-class announcements, engagement party, wedding shower, and all that?" I held onto his forearm and moved my thumb back and forth.

"Let me make something clear. I don't give a shit about any of that, so if you don't want to, then we won't. I already don't conform to the socialite protocol." His voice was filled with something I couldn't place, but when he looked at me, there was hope shining in his eyes. "We will only do what we want to do. I don't have that many friends in the ranks, so it really doesn't matter."

I tilted my head to the side and studied him as the sexiest smirk I had seen on him in days crossed his face. "I don't need to announce it to anyone. I'd be fine with just having a Judge sign the paperwork, have the lawyers finish putting your new name on everything, and be done with it. I know you, though. You want to celebrate and have a party. Have our friends come out and see your brother? Do something."

"What about Malk? Your other friends too. I'm sure there are lots of people I need to meet."

"You've already met Malk, and you know about Dustin. They are the only ones that really matter."

"But I haven't met him." I sat up and faced him. "I would like to have the perfect wedding day, but only if you want to. I can let that go, if you are wholly opposed to a big event."

"The wedding isn't the part that I'm opposed to. I can't wait for the day where I can legally call you Mrs. Allen. When the steward called you Mrs. Allen, you have no idea the kind of manly pride that went through me at that. To have my name attached to you. Fuck, it makes me so Gods dammed happy." He let out a long breath as he said, "I just want to love and protect you, sweetheart. A wedding is going to create a media shitstorm. I don't want them to ruin the day for you."

Rylie was always looking out for me. He was always concerned about me and my feelings. Yet, he didn't appear to think about how important he was to me. I got up and straddled him, rolling my hips against him, until there was a wicked moan that came from him. "You know what I was thinking when that gun was pointed at me?"

His throat bobbed up and down a few times, and I saw the fear in his eyes again. I kissed his cheek and said, "My only regret was that I hadn't walked down the aisle with you yet. That my legal name wasn't Luci Allen."

Rylie blinked, then pulled me close to him and kissed me. He stripped my sweater off me, and then clothes flew through the car. When he entered me, it was quick and with a force that rocked me to my bones. I moaned at the instant fullness of him within me. He held onto my hips as I rolled and ground against him. His lips were trailing down my neck as he said, "I will never announce you as anything else ever again." He lifted me and then slammed me down on his cock. "We will set up a small ceremony, do it somewhere quiet and out of the way. Make it legal."

Thrust.

"Let you have your day."

Thrust.

"Have the officiator bind you in law and before the Gods."

Thrust. I moaned and said, "And be Mrs. Allen forever."

Rylie's eyes met mine and there was a wicked look in his eye, as he lifted me just slightly and then pounded into me. "Fuck, Rylie." I groaned.

The car shifted to the side as it went around a corner, and Rylie threw out his hand to brace us against the force of it. A voice came through the speaker. "Sorry, Mr. Allen."

Rylie's voice came through huskier than usual as he said, "It's fine. Just get us there in one piece."

"As you wish, Mr. Allen."

No sooner had the speaker cut out, then he moved me to my knees before the seat and bent me over, and entered me from behind. The sounds of our skin connecting echoed through the cab.

When Rylie threaded his fingers through my ponytail, I squealed and met his thrust with one of my own. "That's my good girl. Look at you take my cock."

He reached down and tweaked a nipple, and then a smack sounded through the air. Moments later he was saying, "Cum for me, sweetheart."

Smack after smack rang through the cab as he pounded into me and spanked my ass with each connection. "Rylieeeee." I said as I fell over that edge. He picked up speed and pounded me through my orgasm. Then he was releasing himself into me.

He leaned forward, kissing my shoulder softly. I smiled as I looked back over my shoulder at him. I felt the blush on my cheeks, but just looked back down at the seat. He reached over and grabbed a rag and a water bottle, cleaning me up in the process.

Once we were fully clothed again, he pulled me onto his lap and said, "I love you, sweetheart."

"I love you too."

CHAPTER TWENTY-TWO

When we pulled up to our building, Rylie asked the doorman to bring up our luggage.

"Of course, Mr. Allen."

"Daniel?" The doorman had stopped and turned to Rylie, as he said, "Just leave it in the entry. I'll grab it once I've got her settled."

There was a nod, and then we were waiting for the elevator.

"I'm not sure why I'm so exhausted all of a sudden."

"You've been through a bit, Mrs. Allen." I felt his chuckle and couldn't help but smile as I curled up next to his chest.

"When did you get this strong, Rylie?" I whispered against his chest. The deep chuckle from him had me kicking my head up as it sent a jolt through me and settling right on my clit. I squeezed my legs together, and he chuckled again. I couldn't hold back the needy whimper that came out. Gods. Would I ever get enough of this man?

When he stepped out of the elevator, I tried to lower my legs, but he held them tight against him.

"Rylie. I am capable of walking." I said wearily. He simply backed against the main door, which unlocked with a click, and carried me into the condo.

"Welcome Home, Sweetheart."

"I like the sound of that." I said, but when I went to move my legs so he could put me down, he gripped me tighter, and said, "Nope. I'm putting you to bed properly."

"Rylie."

"Yes, Mrs. Allen?" His voice was husky and deep, and I squirmed under him.

"You say that, and I'm not so sure sleep is going to be on the schedule."

"I thought you were exhausted?"

I hummed as I fingered the buttons on his shirt and popped them open. His steps came faster and then he threw me on the bed, and as I bounced, he ripped his shirt off, and tossed his pants onto the floor, before crawling up toward me.

I watched each movement and admired the way that his muscles moved and shifted under his skin. I reached down and unbuttoned my pants, but Rylie's hands were there, making quick work of them. He kissed me quickly as his fingers hooked under the waistband and jerked my pants off my hips.

"You can't be ready to go already, Mr. Allen." I said breathlessly, as he kissed my hip, and then down my thigh as he pulled my pants off my legs and tossed them on the floor. When he tossed them off to the side, his eyes met mine, and he sat up, and proved to me just how wrong I was in that statement. His cock stood proud and as I bit my lower lip and looked up at him through my lashes, he cocked an eyebrow at me as if to say, 'What was that?'

"Hmm…" I reached down and threw my shirt off, while Rylie unhooked my bra and it joined the rest of my clothes on the floor. He grabbed my ankles, tugging, so that I was laying down and spread my legs wide. I reached down and ran my own finger in through some of the cum that had leaked out from our time in the limo, and circled my clit.

"Fuck, Luce." His eyes were wholly focused on me working myself. He stroked himself, watching me, and I leaned my head back and grabbed my breast and pinched my nipple. I moaned, and the next thing I knew, Rylie was removing my fingers and running his tongue down the length of me, before latching onto that bundle of nerves and circling his tongue and flicking it.

Rylie devoured me. Without warning, his fingers slid into me, and I didn't have a chance to wait for permission to cum. There was no holding me back from falling into the pleasure he was providing. Rylie drank up every ounce, and when I came down, he blew on my clit and flicked it with his fingers.

"While you taste delightful, sweetheart, I don't believe I provided you permission to release." There was a devilish smirk on his lips and he crawled up my body, laying open mouthed, tongue swirling kisses all the way up, until he kissed me, and I tasted my release. I could do nothing but moan against him.

His hand trailed down my side, thigh, and gripped onto my knee. Lifting my leg, and standing on his knees, he slid into me painfully slow. "Rylie. No fair being a tease."

"I'm not sure how I'm being a tease." He smirked, but pulled out to just the head of him, and when I moved to have more of him, he slammed into me, and rolled his hips that had him smoothly pulling in and out of me, hitting that spot deep inside.

I grabbed onto the sheets and lifted my hips, meeting his in rhythm. I felt every part of me going taught again, as I whispered, "Rye..."

A soft chuckle came from low in his throat. "Yes, Luci?" I couldn't bring forth a coherent thought as he rolled his hips that had him slowly rubbing against me, causing a heated purr to come from me. Over and over again, he pulsed against that spot, and then just before I lost all sense of reality again, he pulled out and slammed back into me.

I smirked at him, wrapped my legs around him, and rolled him onto his back. "You know, it really isn't fair that you get all the deliciousness."

I slid off him, bent down, running my tongue along the lines of his abs, until I could run my tongue through the slit of his cock. There was a gravelly mummer of my name, as his hips lifted, but I wasn't going to give him what he wanted just yet. My tongue flicked that spot under the rim of him and then I trailed the line of pre-cum that came forth to my lips, letting it hang there between us.

I looked up at Rylie, who was staring at me in aww. "God, that is so fucking sexy."

I licked it up, and then took both of his balls into my mouth, sucking and rolling them. I wrapped my hand around the head of him and pumped him in short strokes. His hips moved, and when I hummed into his balls, his cock twitched.

"Fuck, Luci, I'm not going to last much longer if you keep that up."

After releasing him with a pop, he lifted his hips with a groan as if he were chasing my lips. Slowly, I crawled up him so I straddled him again, rotating my hips so that he was fully seated within me again.

"Good God, Luce." Rylie moaned as I rolled my hips again, and his fingers tightened on me. I bent down to kiss him, and before I could sit back up, he had both of my breasts in his hands and was running his tongue along one nipple.

Moments later, I felt my orgasm building, and I heard Rylie say, "That's my good girl. Fuck me, sweetheart. Cum for me and scream my name."

When he bit down on my nipple, he slapped my ass, hard, and that was all it took for the world to shatter around me. A hoarse, "Rylie!" burst from me, and when he groaned and thrust through my pussy gripping his cock, he exploded with my name, the sound spilling into the air around us.

I collapsed on top of him, sweat coating us both. I may have dozed off momentarily, before he slowly slid me off to the side and went to the bathroom. I vaguely remembered him cleaning me up before wrapping me back up in his arms and saying, "Welcome home, Mrs. Lucille Adaline Allen."

I chuckled and curled up against him. "Welcome home, Rye."

THE END

About the Author

Kimberly M. Ringer lives in Santa Cruz, California with her husband, little human, and two furballs, Wall-E (a Jack Russell mix) and Pippin (a Pomeranian Terrier mix). When she isn't writing, she is reading, playing with the dogs, playing video games or down at the beach. She's a bit geeky and nerdy, so sci-fi references and other things going on in the science world will often end up in her stories.

Contact Kimberly M. Ringer:
www.kimberlymringer.com
Instagram: @kimberlymringer

Facebook: https://www.facebook.com/kimberlymringer

Sign up for my newsletter on my website and receive freebies, coupon codes, and stay up to date on all things Kimberly M. Ringer and K.M. Ringer
Newsletter Signup

Books by
Kimberly M. Ringer

<u>The Five Angels Series</u>
The Five Angels
The Ash'bani
The Helena Crystal

Duchess' Crown
Duchess' Throne

<u>Ashstrike Sanctorum Series</u>
The Ashstrike Sanctorum:
The origin Story
The Astral's Bonded
The Exorci's Touch
My Kismot Savior
the Kismot's Undesirable
The Therugi's Shiver
The Puroklet's Storm (2024)

<u>The Weekend Series</u>
Weekend with Rylie
Weekend with Malcom
Weekend with Desiree (2024)
Weekend with Bethany (2024/25)

<u>Stand Alones</u>
Ashes and Flame
Ceaser's Rainbow (2024/25)

www.ingramcontent.com/pod-product-compliance
Lightning Source LLC
Chambersburg PA
CBHW061447210726

48287CB00007B/2390